NOVA

Look for other books by Chuck Black

The Kingdom Series
Kingdom's Dawn
Kingdom's Hope
Kingdom's Edge
Kingdom's Call
Kingdom's Quest
Kingdom's Reign

The Knights of Arrethtrae
Sir Kendrick and the Castle of Bel Lione
Sir Bentley and Holbrook Court
Sir Dalton and the Shadow Heart
Lady Carliss and the Waters of Moorue
Sir Quinlan and the Swords of Valor
Sir Rowan and the Camerian Conquest

The Wars of the Realm
Cloak of the Light
Rise of the Fallen
Light of the Last

The Starlore Legacy
Nova
Flight
Lore
Oath
Merchant
Reclamation
Creed
Journey
Crucible
Covenant
Revolution
Maelstrom

www.ChuckBlack.com

THE STARLORE LEGACY

NOVA

EPISODE ONE

CHUCK BLACK

PERFECT
PRAISE
PUBLISHING

Nova

Cover design ©2019 by Elena Karoumpali
Illustrations ©2019 by Chuck Black

Published by Perfect Praise Publishing
Williston, North Dakota

ISBN 978-0-9915735-2-3

Printed in the United States of America

Library of Congress Control Number: 2019911610

CONTENTS

PROLOGUE

Ancient Days

S omething was drawing her to them, and she didn't know why—the stars. An inexplicable tether tugged on the corner of her mind. Though brilliant in their innumerable glory, something was out of place, and even at her youthful age she knew it. The stars of the Aurora Galaxy beckoned, daring her to dream, and dream she did. Brae's imagination both delighted and frustrated her. "A journey of a thousand miles doesn't begin with one step," her father had said. "It begins with a dream."

Often in the middle of the night, Brae would climb out of her window onto the roof, lay back, and gaze for hours at the endless sea of stars. There was an ache in her heart she couldn't explain. She felt left out, bypassed, and confined by life, school, and the duties of their country home.

Tonight the stars shone more brilliantly than she ever remembered.

"If only—"

"If only?"

Brae looked over at the open window she had escaped through just an hour earlier.

"Dad, you're still awake?"

"Yes, but why are you?" He glanced up at the stars. "Ah...I see," he said with a smile. Elias Thornton climbed out the window and lay down next to his daughter.

Brae giggled.

"The night is too beautiful to miss out on a good star-gazing," Elias said. "Most twelve-year olds are fast asleep by now."

Brae shook her head. "Not this one." She reached for his hand. "Do you think everyone likes to look at the stars?" Brae asked.

"Perhaps, but not as much as we do."

Brae looked at a brilliant cluster of stars directly above them, right next to the Omega Nebula.

"I want to go there," Brae said, pointing at the sparkling bright jewels. She sighed deeply. "But I think that instead I shall live and die a lowly country girl."

Elias laughed. "I think you've been reading too many theatrical classics of the ancient days. Listen, Brae, you were born for something great, and it's your understanding of the truth that will lead you to it."

"But we live in the country, Dad. How can anything great ever be done from here?"

"Sovereign Ell Yon knows who you are and where you are. When the time is right, he'll call for you."

Brae looked over at her father, unconvinced. She was coming to the age when she was beginning to question everything, even the things her father taught her. Even though her father's version of the ancient days was vastly different than what others believed, a ring of truth was underlying in everything he said. But how could a simple man who lived in the outlying lands know the plans of the great Ell Yon?

"Today at school, Aubin said that the Immortals were just a myth."

"I see, and what did you say?"

Brae hesitated. "I told him he was wrong."

Elias looked at Brae and raised an eyebrow.

"I did," she smiled sheepishly, "but I said some other things too."

"I can only imagine," Elias responded quietly.

"Why does no one else believe as we do?" Brae asked.

Elias sat up and Brae joined him. He looked deep into her eyes as if wanting to make sure she would really listen. "Because the truth of the ancient days was passed down through our family for thousands of years, untainted by the speculations of those who have lost faith in Ell Yon and the Immortals."

Brae thought about his explanation for a moment, imagining a hundred forefathers telling their children the stories that her father had told her time and again. She never grew weary of hearing them.

"If only we could travel through time and see for ourselves!" Brae's face lit up as she thought of the adventure of such a journey.

"Time travel is possible," Elias stated.

"Sure it is," Brae replied, unable to hide her cynicism.

"It's true, but only in one direction. Think about it; we are traveling through time right now. It's possible to travel forward through time and at different speeds. But time travel is always a one-way ticket. You can never go back."

"That doesn't help much," Brae complained, hunching her shoulders.

"One day it will, but for now it's time for you to climb back in bed."

Brae grabbed her father's arm. "Please just a little longer. Tell me once more of the ancient days."

Elias hesitated then kissed the top of Brae's head.

She looked up at her father and smiled. Then she snuggled under his arm, waiting to hear the story once more. Elias drew in a long breath.

"The quest for immortality became an obsession, not just for a few or for the wealthy, but for all of humanity." Elias spoke as if he were reading a drama, and Brae loved it. "Science was the key...the hope and inspiration of mankind. The discipline had nearly doubled the average lifespan of the healthy, but it was never enough. It would never be enough. A dozen worlds grasped for immortality, but like sand through fingers, the ever-elusive quest could not be fulfilled."

Elias held out his hand and slowly closed it. Brae imagined streams of sand slipping through his fingers

"Every brilliant scientist across the Aurora Galaxy clung to the promise of Deitum Prime, the genetic code-altering agent offered to humanity as a promise from one of two alien races that were indeed immortal. Ancient legends tell of one Torian ambassador that had visited and given hope to mankind on the blissful world of Mesos, once thought to be the cradle of humanity. One vial of the promised agent was injected into the bloodstream of a man, and the journey to promised immortality began."

Elias paused in his narration and glanced over at Brae. She was deep in thought, lost to her own musings about what her father had just said. She slowly looked up at him.

"What is Deitum Prime, Dad? Really."

Elias waited...wondering how much a young girl of Brae's age could understand. But she was bright beyond her years.

"Deitum Prime is alien bio-technology. When it was introduced to Mesos, it quickly had a global impact, which soon spread to other star systems. In truth, this self-replicating agent has the ability to alter the genetic code of anyone who is exposed to it. The agent is so complex that in spite of thousands of years of research, we still don't fully understand how it works. Because of the promise of immortality, replication plants were built to speed up the production and dissemination of Deitum Prime throughout the galaxy. Does that help?"

Brae nodded solemnly. "I think so." Then she smiled. "Continue!"

"The initial results were beyond anything the galaxy could have imagined. Improved strength, knowledge, and sensory stimulation were just three of the enhancements agent Deitum Prime provided. A race between worlds erupted to fulfill the immortality quest first, and great battles were fought because of it. The replication plants helped spread Deitum Prime to all of humanity. By means of crops, water, and atmospheric seeding, Deitum Prime began to transform the entire human race with the hope of full and complete genetic code alteration, thereby transforming mankind to the status of the Immortals."

Elias paused. Here the drama became more real. Brae could feel the shift in her father's words. This is where the history of a galaxy somehow became personal.

"But out of this galactic effort to elevate mankind to the status of the Immortals and its resulting wars rose a race of people that resisted, and they were hated for it. By galactic standards, the Rayleans were small and inconsequential, yet one day the fate of the entire galaxy would rest on the shoulders of this obscure and rebellious people. But it would take the influence of a powerful Immortal and a willing leader to make it so..."

CHAPTER

1

Pure Flight

Anti-graviton — an elementary particle that
mediates a force equal and opposite to that of a
graviton and its force of normal gravity. The
anti-graviton is a massless, stable particle that
travels at the speed of light.

Daeson stood on the edge of the canyon wall, the toes of his propulsion boots hanging just beyond the granite edge that separated the expanse of the canyon from the solid ground upon which he stood. Breathtaking! He could feel his stomach flip as he anticipated his leap into the empty cavern of air. He wondered if his companions felt it too.

He looked to his left. Xandra was outfitted in her skin-tight black wing suit. A tuft of fiery red hair was visible between her cheekbone and the pad of her helmet. She smiled at him, nodded and flipped down her visor. Just beyond her, Daeson could see Linden doing a last-minute check on his wing suit, extending his arms and visually checking for any tears or fraying of the wing material. Like Xandra, he too possessed the superior physique of a finely tuned muscular body.

Linden glanced toward Xandra and Daeson and nodded. An early release from classes at the academy and the calm late afternoon air made the timing for this jump perfect. What they were about to do was as close to pure flying as possible.

"You cadets ready for this?" Linden's voice burst through Daeson's helmet audio.

Daeson flipped his visor down, and amber symbology immediately populated the left and right of his visor, giving him altitude, speed, wind, coordinates, flight path, and a variety of other information needed for the jump.

"Ready," Daeson replied.

"Let's do this!" Xandra chimed in.

"You're sure you checked the anti-graviton density on the landing field?"

Xandra flipped up her visor, put her hands on her hips, tilted her head and glared at Daeson.

He tried to suppress a broad smile but couldn't. He pointed at her and laughed. The smirk on her face transformed into a wry smile. She had initiated this jump, along with many of their other "risky" adventures. As daring as she was, she was always thorough in her preparation.

Daeson could barely make out the pin-sized landing site far below and way off in the distance down the broad canyon...much too far to make with just a wing suit. The propulsion boots gave them the extra speed they would need to make the jump, and of course there was always the backup parachute. This would be their fourth jump but the furthest attempt yet, so they had plotted out their flight profile in detail.

Since this jump was risky, there was too much to lose to leave anything to chance, especially for Linden. As the next in line for ruler of the Jyptonian government, all risks were calculated risks. That this endeavor was unsanctioned made it all the more tempting and thrilling. But what really made this jump so exhilarating would be the landing. They had discovered a rare anti-graviton field that spanned six sections of land. In other regions of the planet, they were more common, but here on the southern continent, such a field was unusual.

Like most anti-graviton sites, the inverted gravity field was circular, with the greatest intensity of anti-gravitons in the center, diminishing toward the edges. A stone thrown into the field would fly upward but always return slowly to the ground as it traveled outward to the field's perimeter, where normal gravity gradually overtook the anti-graviton field.

What this meant for Daeson, Linden, and Xandra was that if they hit the front of the field at the right speed, angle, and altitude, they could affect a landing on the far side of the field without deploying a chute. Entering the anti-graviton field at ninety miles per hour, flying upward two-hundred feet, and then moments later slipping down the far side of the field to land gently on their feet would be a rush. No thrill on Jypton could compare.

Anti-graviton fields existed in other regions of Jypton, overlapping one another and resulting in gravity suspension pockets. Daeson had only seen them from a distance. These floating islands rich with vegetation and even animal life created miniature eco systems. In one region on the northern continent, hundreds of floating islands were suspended at various elevations above the ground. The discovery of the anti-graviton was also at the heart of much of the planet's transportation system.

"Last one to land buys at the club tonight!" Linden radioed then spread his arms and fell off the canyon wall. Daeson and Xandra wasted no time in following him downward at dizzying speeds, skimming close to the jagged canyon walls until enough velocity gave them the ability to "fly." Within seconds, the three friends were screaming through the vastness of the canyon air. Daeson felt the wind push against him as he turned and maneuvered, edging closer to three large rocky spires jutting upward from the canyon floor.

"Move over!" Xandra's voice was slightly muffled as she dove below Daeson and closer to the approaching spires.

"Don't be foolish, Xandra!" Daeson warned.

"We can't deviate much from the profile, or we won't make the landing site," Linden called out.

"You boys are such killjoys!" Xandra countered.

Daeson checked his flight parameters and compared them with the optimal flight path depicted on his visor. He did a quick mental calculation then altered his flight to follow Xandra. Linden followed a few seconds later. The rocky spires grew to gigantic proportions in seconds as the three human wind surfers screamed toward them at over one hundred twenty miles an hour. They whizzed by the ominous formations, and Daeson's stomach rose up to his throat. That was closer than he had anticipated.

"Woohoo!" He heard Linden and Xandra scream almost simultaneously.

When they diverted back to the planned course, they were only thirty feet low on their profile.

"It's time to fire the propulsion boots. Do a full twenty-second burn to recover lost altitude," Linden radioed. "Three...two...one...fire!"

Daeson made tight fists on both hands at the same time and felt his boot thrusters ignite. The velocity kick was empowering. As he and Linden accelerated forward and upward, Daeson caught a glimpse of Xandra out of the corner of his eye as she veered off to his right.

"I've got a problem," Xandra radioed.

"What's up, Xandra?" Linden called.

"One of my propulsion boots won't ignite...trying again." A second later..."No go!"

"Get back on course and gain as much altitude as you can," Daeson radioed.

"Already on it," Xandra replied.

"It won't matter," Linden interrupted. "You won't have enough speed and altitude to make the landing site. You need to slow to chute deployment speed and abort."

"I can make it," Xandra radioed.

Daeson quickly shut down his boot thrusters with a few seconds of burn time left.

"No you won't. Don't be foolish, Xandra! Abort!" Linden's voice was strained, his feelings for her exposed with each clipped warning.

Daeson spotted the landing site ahead. Linden was higher and further because of his full burn, but Daeson's own flight path showed that he could make it. He would enter the anti-graviton field a little steeper and lower than he wanted to, and the landing might be a bit rough, but it would still be safe. He waited for Xandra's reply.

"Xandra!" Linden shouted over the com.

"My problem just got worse. No chute," Xandra radioed. Daeson heard uncharacteristic apprehension in her voice.

Three seconds of silence sobered the thrill-seeking trio instantly.

"What's your profile show?" Linden asked.

"It's calculating that I'll hit the anti-graviton field thirty feet in at one-eighty." Pause. "Thirty-eight degrees."

They all knew that with such momentum and at that angle, the anti-graviton field would only soften her impact with the ground. If she survived, it would then throw her like a rag doll hundreds of feet into the air and probably beyond the effects of the anti-graviton field and into normal gravity, where she would impact the ground a second time and with deadly force.

"Try your chute again," Daeson instructed, simultaneously preparing for his own landing.

"No good. I'm just going to have to make the landing," Xandra replied.

Daeson thought quickly. The silence from Linden told him his cousin was scrambling for a solution too, but their options were limited if not nil, and time was short. The thrill in Daeson's stomach turned to nausea.

"Keep over the dark terrain as much as possible to capitalize on any updrafts," Linden finally said.

"At those entry parameters, what side of the anti-graviton field will she exit?" Daeson asked Linden.

Two precious seconds passed as Linden calculated. "It's fifty-fifty."

"You land on the far side, and I'll land on the near," Daeson said. He carried his speed a little longer since he was already low, then began flaring for his entry.

"Got it," Linden said.

"Get to the field, Xandra. We'll be there for you," Daeson promised.

"And do what?" she countered. "Catch me?"

There was no response. What could they say? Daeson figured he had less than a minute to land and prepare for Xandra's entry. Just ahead he saw Linden adjust his course slightly upward, then enter the anti-graviton field as planned. It was an odd site to watch him plummet nearly one hundred feet downward, slowing rapidly before reversing direction upward. Seconds later, Linden was "sliding" down the seam between normal gravity and the bubble of the anti-gravity field. He landed softly on the far side. Now it was Daeson's turn.

Daeson entered the site faster and much closer to the near side of the anti-graviton field. He felt the deceleration instantly, but wondered if he was going to impact the ground before reversing upward. Just thirty feet from the ground, his velocity came to zero, and then he began accelerating upward. But unlike Linden, his horizontal movement reversed, and the anti-graviton field threw him upward and back in the direction from which he had come. His landing on the near side was not as smooth as Linden's had been. He hit the ground and tumbled. Quickly regaining his footing, he ignored the pain in his right thigh, the result of a small, sharp rock in the path of his tumble. He scanned the sky from the direction he had just come and spotted Xandra. She was frighteningly low and fast.

"Come on, Xandra," he whispered and ran to align himself with her flight path. He glanced to the far side of the field and saw Linden doing the same.

"It's been nice knowing you guys," Xandra radioed, apprehension now replaced by fear.

"Shut up, Xandra...you're going to make it!" Linden ordered.

She would have to carry her speed to the last moment and flare at exactly the right time. Her descent was frightening to watch. Daeson had never seen such speed so low to the ground before. A lump swelled up in his throat. Even if by some miracle she survived impacting the ground, the second impact from the slingshot throw of the anti-graviton field would surely kill her.

Fifteen seconds before field penetration, Daeson concocted a crazy plan. He withdrew a small knife and cut the webbing between the legs of his wing suit, then ran toward Xandra as she flew over him at blinding speed. Thirty feet out from the anti-graviton field, he turned to see Xandra pierce the anti-graviton semi-sphere too fast, too low and at too steep of an angle. He could hardly watch as she initiated a full body flare with arms and legs spread wide.

Daeson couldn't help but admire her courage because the natural reaction would be to close up and brace for impact. But that was not Xandra. Her deceleration was dramatic, but it wasn't quite enough. She hit the ground, throwing up dust and rocks, which immediately launched upward into the air with her.

With no time to think about her injuries, Daeson sprinted into the anti-graviton field toward her as fast as he could run, knowing that as soon as the field strength equaled his weight, he would be pushed upward. It would not be much, but any extra height he could gain would help. Twenty feet in he felt his feet loosing traction, but his forward momentum carried him onward. He kept his eye on Xandra as the anti-graviton field threw her two hundred feet into the air, upward, outward, and back toward him. Daeson flew upward, twisting his body to aim at the intersecting flight path with Xandra. He couldn't possibly hope to gain enough altitude on his own, but he still had a few seconds of propulsion time left on his boot thrusters.

He had one shot. Daeson aimed and ignited the boosters.

Xandra was twisting about, trying to position herself for some sort of crash fall when she saw Daeson. At least she was conscious and able to respond to his desperate rescue attempt. His boot thrusters, coupled with the anti-graviton push, propelled him toward his helpless companion. It would be close.

At the pinnacle of Xandra's launch back and out of the anti-graviton field, the fury of speed and disaster seemed suspended for a few seconds as Daeson reached for her. She was just inches from his grasp. He stretched—she stretched—it was just enough. Fingers grasped, then hands latched onto each other's forearms, and Daeson pulled her close. Xandra's usually fearless gaze was not fearless in this moment...not now. The expression was brief, but Daeson had never seen her so vulnerable...so hopeful in another. Her right cheek was bleeding from her impact with the ground just seconds earlier.

"What now, brainiac?" Xandra asked as they began free-falling arm in arm from one hundred fifty feet. "We both die?"

"Hang on tight!" Daeson shouted.

Xandra hugged him tightly as he pulled the ripcord on his chute. Getting a full chute at this altitude would be nearly impossible, but their chutes were designed for extreme low altitude deployment by use of a small charge. Daeson hoped it would be enough.

The ground rushed up at them at gut-wrenching speed until he felt the jarring force of an opening chute on his harness with only twenty feet remaining. Adrenaline kept their embrace from breaking as the full force of the chute tried to pull them apart. A fraction of a second later, they hit the ground with a thud. There was no chance of executing a reasonable parachute landing, so they both had enough sense to push away from each other and roll with the impact.

Daeson felt the crushing force of normal gravity punch the air from his lungs as a shock wave of pain flowed across his bones and muscles. In the aftermath, he lay still on his back for a moment, trying to recover his air and analyzing his pain to see if anything was broken. When he thought he might pass out for lack of oxygen, his lungs yielded and filled. He gasped to restore his sense of being then slowly rolled onto his left side to locate Xandra. She was face down and turned away from him, motionless. Had she survived? He tried to lift himself up but could not garner the strength.

Heavy boots striking the ground in fast succession filtered through the ringing in Daeson's ears. He tried to call to Xandra; then he saw Linden slide to a dusty halt where she lay. He gently rolled her onto her back, and she remained motionless. Daeson forced himself to crawl toward them. He rose up on an elbow to see if Xandra was alive.

Linden's gaze didn't break from the motionless girl's face. "Xandra," he pleaded, carefully touching her cheek.

Slowly she opened her eyes and moaned.

"Ugh...I hurt everywhere!" she murmured, a wisp of a smile forming on her lips.

It was all Daeson needed. He rolled to his back and took a deep breath. He heard Xandra respond with a chuckle, and he couldn't help countering with his own truncated laughter. Then Linden added an emotional sigh. Soon the three of them were laughing uncontrollably. Deep down, Daeson knew his response was the result of fear, having been pushed to the very brink of death.

CHAPTER

2

The Elite

Stasis Field – a photonic force designed to enhance and strengthen the material with which it is engaged. The force perimeter can be shaped to create a molecular-level cutting edge that can penetrate most materials, excluding another stasis field.

The sweet aroma of fried mutton enticed Daeson to wake up. He slowly opened his eyes and felt the cool morning breeze glide across his bruised body as the gentle cooing of mourning doves eased his mind into full consciousness. He stretched and squinted, allowing the first rays of Jypton's giant sun to further cast away the shadows of sleep. His sore muscles screamed against any movement, a reminder that the previous day's adventure was not a dream. He was grateful that this morning was one he could look forward to, considering the alternative of yesterday's outcome. A quiet knock only slightly preceded the near-silent retreat of his chamber's door.

"Master Daeson, the morning meal is prepared." A stately middle-aged man entered, carrying a dark blue flight suit draped across his left forearm. "You are scheduled for flight training this morning, tech academics and Talon training in the afternoon."

"I know my schedule, Tuvi," Daeson said through a yawn. "And I really wish you wouldn't barge into my room like that."

"Forgive me, Master Daeson, but your mother's command overrules your wishes. I believe it has something to do with your consistent inability to present yourself at the morning meal in a timely fashion."

Tuvi laid the flight suit across the foot of the bed and stood staring expectantly at Daeson, who moaned and rolled over. As an upper classman, he was not required to stay at the academy, and why would he with such luxuries waiting for him at home.

"I hate you, Tuvi."

"Yes, sir."

"And I suppose you're not leaving until I'm dressed."

"I have my orders, Master Daeson."

Daeson sighed, then swung his legs over the side of the bed. He noticed that Tuvi was eyeing his scrapes and bruises suspiciously.

He looked at Tuvi and raised one eyebrow. "Not a word," he commanded.

Tuvi sighed and shook his head in disapproval.

The room gleamed with a beautiful mixture of ancient splendor and modern technology. When the Immortals had begun interacting with humankind thousands of years earlier, the infusion of technology had been so rapid that an intriguing blend of the ancient medieval world and the modern was created.

Two small bots whooshed through the open door, hovering close to the ground. They began scanning and cleaning the room as Daeson forced himself to stand. He stretched once more while looking at Tuvi out of the corner of his eye.

"I'm up, Tuvi. You can go now!"

A smirk flashed across the servant's face. Tuvi then turned and left the room. Daeson finished stretching then fell back onto the silky soft bed that beckoned his return. He smiled. The world was perfect... yet something deep in a remote corner of his mind whispered otherwise.

Daeson's father, Pierce Lockridge, had been second only to his older brother, Chancellor Marcus Lockridge, in the royal Jyptonian family. When Daeson was just a boy, his father had become ill and died. The Chancellor offered Daeson's mother and him frequent access to the palace, which allowed the Chancellor's son, Linden, and Daeson to spend countless hours together in study and play. The two had grown up nearly as brothers, with an extra edge of competitiveness that Daeson tried to quell. But it often got the best of him in spite of his mother's admonishments. As the boys entered the later teen years, their competitiveness only grew, and Daeson sensed a rising animosity in Linden, especially if ever Daeson outperformed his cousin. It was a delicate rope he had to walk.

As a member of the royal family, Daeson lived a life of privilege and opportunity that was the envy of all of the Elite. And although his acceptance into the Starcraft Academy was a given, he had proven to be a very skilled pilot in his own right. Not even the nay-sayers of the Royal privileged could deny his position as one of the top cadets, especially when it came to piloting skills. Only Linden himself could claim a better performance.

Daeson yearned for something he could never have: his father's watching him enter and graduate from the academy. He often imagined the look of pride on his face. And so Daeson found solace in the reserved yet quietly enthusiastic attention of his mother.

Daeson looked toward the doorway, wondering if Tuvi would reappear to check on his progress. The image on one of the wall displays near the doorway was filled with a picture of Linden and Daeson kneeling before the carcass of a spiny Kolazo beast. Jypton was the only habitable planet of the Nyson System. Its atmosphere, oceans, and various ecosystems allowed for thousands of species of life to flourish, including the dangerous Kolazo beasts.

Kolazo hunting was a tradition of the royal family, one of the more dangerous sports they were allowed to participate in. Kolazo beasts were not indigenous to the southern continent, but a desire for such thrilling sport initiated a transplant of the creature from the western continent.

Here the Kolazo topped the food chain, for it was a fearsome beast, weighing three times more than a man, with a thick, tough hide. Its front legs were powerful and slightly longer than the hind legs. A large gator-type mouth with sharp teeth all around, coupled with horny spines protruding backward from its spine, demanded the respect of even the most experienced hunters. Hoofed feet allowed the beast to cover short distances incredibly fast. Outrunning the creature without an aerobike was simply not an option. Its aggressive look belied its true demeanor, however, as Kolazos were typically reclusive animals unless provoked.

Hunting was one such way to provoke the Kolazo, so the courage of a rising prince was thoroughly tested by the activity since the only weapon allowed was a Talon. Both Daeson and Linden loved hunting the Kolazo. Other less daunting species filled the plains, forests, skies, and oceans with colorful life that was a sight to behold. For the most part, the people of Jypton lived in harmony with their non-human cohabiters.

Daeson met Tuvi halfway down the stairs. By the look on his face, Daeson could tell Tuvi had been berated by his mother for allowing Daeson to escape the beginning of the meal once more. Daeson winked as he passed. Tuvi sighed, spun about and followed. On Jypton a perfectly balanced caste culture had developed among the people, dating back nearly 3000 years. The ancient days, nearly forgotten, had forged a society that flowed in harmonious production and advancement. At least that was the perspective of the Elite, the ruling class of Jyptonians, including the royal family, which controlled all seats of power throughout the world.

The Elite oligarchy was tightly defined, and their rule was complete. The masses who were not part of the Elite were referred to as the Colloquials, but even they were considered privileged by galactic standards. However, the Drudge caste, to which Tuvi belonged, turned the gears of the Jyptonian culture machine. Composed almost exclusively of Rayleans, this race of people had been offered refuge over a millennium earlier when they fled the disintegration of a neighboring star system. Their robust work ethic and innate ability to adapt and improve technology quickly won them a place on the planet as a people that offered the Jyptonian world a hearty industry and technology base.

Over the centuries the culture evolved, the Raylean population grew, and the Elite became nervous. Laws and hierarchal governments were established to limit the offices that could be held by the Rayleans. Travel restrictions, income ceilings, and weapons possession limitations invariably created a near indentured servitude society ruled exclusively by the Jyptonian Elite. In time, the Rayleans didn't have the capacity to escape the chains of poverty and restraint the Jyptonians had shackled upon them.

Saskia Lockridge greeted her son with a kiss as he entered the dining hall.

"You look stunning this morning, dear mother!" Daeson said. He hugged her, then escorted her back to her chair. "I believe today you are the envy of all Jypton."

Saskia smiled. "Don't think for an instant that your charm will excuse you for being late to breakfast again."

"I wouldn't think of it," Daeson said as he reached for a plate of seasoned fried mutton.

Saskia handed him a bowl of delicious red, orange, and blue fruit. "The trunket berries are especially rich in Deitum Prime. Make sure you keep up with your daily quota. Tuvi, give him a supplemental dosage."

"Yes, my lady."

Daeson hurried his breakfast so he wouldn't have to speed too much on his aerobike. His aerobike used the same technology that most transportation vehicles employed...grav-tech, a technology resulting from the discovery of the anti-graviton particle. Although many craft used full thrust-powered engines to fly through the atmosphere with ease, vehicles equipped with grav-tech was the most efficient and cleanest method of transportation. A vehicle with grav-tech could hover a short distance off the ground but not technically fly. This did limit most of Jypton's transportation to two-dimensional travel, but it was a trade they were willing to make to keep the airways free from congestion and pollution.

Daeson engaged the grav-engine and felt the aerobike lift smoothly into the air. Before the sleek machine was fully elevated, he pushed the throttles up and was skimming across the palace yard faster than he should have. Once he was on the streets of the city, he accelerated even further.

Athlone, Jypton's capital, was a majestic and regal city with a multi-millennial heritage. Its ancient architects were master artisans that passed on a reverence for their work through the guild responsible for city design. A perfectly balanced integration of advanced technology embraced the massive stone and marbled structures from the echoes of the past. Gleaming towers and sprawling gardens decorated the cityscape throughout its broad expanse.

Only one section of the city didn't seem to belong: Drudgetown, a large and expanding suburb of Athlone southeast of the city, housed a majority of the Drudge caste. The Jyptonian's need for service did not keep pace with the growing population of the Drudge caste, and measures had been taken in times past to remedy the problem. Even still, Drudgetown was an ever-increasing smudge on the beauty of Athlone and a great source of discord for the citizens of the capital. Athlone was not alone. Five other major cities of Jypton had their own Drudgetowns. The Jyptonians were anxious about integrating too many Drudges into their society, and because the Rayleans refused to adopt the Deitum Prime solution to their physical limitations, segregation was inevitable.

Daeson wasted no time in traversing the western district of the city and arrived at the academy with a few minutes to spare.

One fourth of Daeson's academy class was composed of the Elite class. They would be selected to lead the rest of the Jyptonian Planetary Aero Forces. The remaining cadets would be the Colloquials. This structure was repeated throughout all of the segments of the Jyptonian military and academic institutions. A constant, unspoken animosity existed between the classes, especially when a Colloquial proved worthy of higher rank because of his or her skill. But because the system worked, nearly every citizen of Jypton respected the system. In spite of this animosity, Daeson had a way with the Colloquials that was unique.

In the past, members of the royal family had sometimes attended the academy, but it was not encouraged simply because of the risks involved. When the Royals did attend, special provisions were made to ensure their safety. In spite of much dissuasion, Daeson and Linden had agreed as boys that they would join and become the greatest Starcraft pilots Jypton had ever seen. And though both had entered the academy as young men, Daeson's enthusiasm to fly had brought them there.

To Daeson, the T32 Starcraft was a twin-engine machine of pure engineering beauty and marvel. He remembered as a lad watching a Starcraft split the sky above with its sleek and deadly form and being inexplicably drawn to it...to pilot it. There was an ache in his heart that he couldn't explain nor dismiss, an ache that grew within him—until his first flight. Within the first ten minutes, he knew he was born to pilot a Starcraft. It was in his genetics, with or without the Deitum Prime. He had come home.

The Starcraft mission for today was practicing slipstream jumps and atmospheric reentry. Daeson was part of a four-ship formation led by instructor pilot Nawlin. Three cadet pilots would fill out the rest of the formation. Number two in the flight was Xandra Savil, his thrill-seeking accomplice. Recognized for holding her own against the best of the cadets, she was an Elite that Daeson and Linden had known since they were children.

Her family was one of the few ruling families the Chancellor relied on to govern Jypton. That Daeson's cousin, Linden, would court and marry Xandra was an unspoken expectation, but something seemed to hinder the relationship. Though Xandra had been careful through the years, Daeson suspected that her affections had fallen on him and not Linden. And he suspected Linden felt it too, for he had not pursued Xandra even though he was drawn to her. Neither did Daeson pursue Xandra out of respect for his cousin and the royal family.

As beautiful as she was, Daeson dared not touch that which would surely be forbidden. This ever-present relational tension was awkward at first, but it had become the norm, and each played their role eloquently. Daeson wondered how yesterday's brush with death and his rescue of Xandra would affect this delicate balance they had lived with for so long. In the back of Daeson's mind, he wondered if Xandra was really fit to fly today considering what she had just been through. She would never let on to the extent of her injury, but other than a slight limp that only he and Linden would notice, she seemed fine.

Daeson, as number three in the flight, would assume the flight-lead for number four. The fourth pilot was Silax Tigratinna, a blond haired Colloquial cadet. He went by the nickname Tig.

"Viper flight, assume loose fingertip formation for slipstream jump," commanded instructor Nawlin.

The three Starcraft vessels spread the formation so that they were a comfortable distance from each other. This would insure there was no wingtip overlap in case they arrived on the other side of the jump at slightly different times.

Although this was Daeson's first piloted slipstream jump, he had experienced the technology many times before. As a member of the royal family, travel to other planets in their system and beyond was often required.

The technology of slipstream jumping dated back thousands of years. A system of hyperspace conduits linked most of the major planets and moons in this region of the galaxy. It was believed that these conduits were not a naturally occurring phenomenon but were actually created by one of the two ancient races of Immortals. Apparently, a relation existed between the mass of a body in space and a slipstream conduit. Nearly every conduit had been discovered and annotated on the master slipstream map shared unilaterally with the civilized planets in the region.

However, large sections of the galaxy were unreachable because the slipstream conduits had been sabotaged by the robots during the Artificial Intelligence or AI Wars, isolating many planets from the rest of humanity. Within a slipstream conduit, the effects of light speed travel are circumvented. Outside of a slipstream conduit, traveling at near light speed causes time to dilate for the traveler. If a vessel were to travel at 99.9% the speed of light for one hour, the passengers on board would age one hour, but the people in the rest of the galaxy would have aged over twenty-two hours.

For long journeys, one might arrive after an entire generation of people had lived and died. The slipstream conduits insulated the travelers from this effect by creating a space-time shroud around the vessel. Additionally, the conduits allow a vessel equipped with a slipstream jump drive to travel at a speed of approximately one light year per second. A vessel could jump from system to system and traverse vast regions of the galaxy in just a few days.

"Prepare to engage slipstream jump drives on my mark."

Their first slipstream jump would take them to the nearest moon of Tiran. This jump would feel nearly instantaneous.

"Three, two, one, engage." For a fraction of a second, Nawlin's command stretched as his Starcraft elongated and then disappeared before him. An instant later, Daeson's Starcraft was in perfect position right and slightly aft of instructor Nawlin, the moon of Tiran brightly gleaming before him. Daeson could never quite get used to the slipstream effect of feeling as though he were in two places at the same time.

Nawlin led the four-ship formation on four more jumps through the Nyson system before arriving back at their home world of Jypton. Now came the second phase of their mission for the day...atmospheric reentry.

"Viper three, assume tactical split for reentry and rejoin in the atmosphere."

"Check," Daeson replied over the com.

Even more advanced than the visor of his jump suit helmet, the visor of his Starcraft helmet displayed all of the flight symbology of the Starcraft's performance.

Only rarely did a pilot need to look down at one of the two glass consoles in the cockpit.

Daeson maneuvered his sleek Starcraft up and away from Viper one and two. Viper four stayed close on his wing in fingertip formation as they spread to a one-mile split to the right of the other two Starcrafts. Daeson took a moment to appreciate the absolute beauty of the blue and white orb beneath them. He had been in space dozens of times, but the splendor of the majestic world from this perch never escaped him.

"Set reentry vector to 5.69 degrees and engage energy shield." Viper one's command shattered Daeson's silent reflection.

"Viper two, check."

"Viper three, check."

"Viper four, check."

"Initiate reentry burn on my mark…three, two, one, engage."

Daeson tapped the glass panel menu that would engage his forward thruster. He felt the Starcraft's deceleration instantly. Daeson knew this was perhaps one of the most precarious aspects of space flight simply because the transition from space to atmosphere required precise calculations of hundreds of variables by the Starcraft's computers and induced tremendous forces on the craft's structure. Upon entering the atmosphere, the Starcraft's atmospheric horizontal and vertical control surfaces would engage. The energy shield or E-shield was the only factor that kept the crafts and pilots from burning to a crisp during the transition. This is why their training required five such missions, of which this was the last for Daeson. His wingman, Tig, had only accomplished reentry once before.

Daeson scanned his visor, as well as his glass displays inside the cockpit. All looked perfect: E-shield at 100% and holding, outer hull temperature at 375°and stable. He glanced over his left shoulder and could see Viper one and Viper two one mile away, the visor conveniently placing a box and tag symbol around them for easy identification. His thoughts turned to Xandra, knowing she would handle her Starcraft perfectly even though it was her first re-entry. The orange glow of their E-shields shrouded the crafts. As he looked over his right shoulder to confirm Viper four's position aft of his wingtip, he was just in time to see the Starcraft pitch slightly downward.

"Viper four, correct your reentry vector. You're too steep," Daeson radioed.

"Roger, Viper three. I seem to have a horizontal stabilizer malfunction."

Daeson could hear the tension in the cadet's voice. With each passing second, the atmosphere became thicker and Viper four's Starcraft pitched steeper and steeper. Daeson adjusted his own reentry vector to keep his wingman in sight.

"Viper four, this is Viper one—attempt manual override."

A long agonizing moment of silence ensued, and Daeson pitched steeper to keep up with Viper four.

"No response," came four's delayed reply. "Attempting system reset."

"Negative, Viper four! I repeat negative! A system reset will drop your E-shield!"

Daeson held his breath, waiting to see if his wingman and his Starcraft would burn up and disintegrate.

"Roger, Viper one," Tig replied.

Daeson exhaled.

"E-shield at 60% and dropping," Viper four replied. "Please advise."

Daeson glanced at his own E-shield status—72%. Their reentry vector was far too steep for the shield to maintain integrity. Daeson waited for Viper one to reply, but the silence told him everything.

"Reattempt manual override," Viper one finally called out.

Daeson could barely make out the bright glow of the two Starcrafts high above them.

"Negative response! Shield at 43%! Hull temperature at..." There was a two-second pause. "...twenty-four hundred degrees."

"Viper four, redirect all system power to the energy shield. This should buy you enough time to make it through reentry."

Daeson did a quick calculation, comparing the rate of Viper four's shield degradation to the time left for reentry...the cadet would never make it.

"Systems are failing! E-shield at 18%! Hull temperature critical!" Viper four's voice was frantic now.

Daeson pushed his Starcraft steeper to stay with his wingman as he awaited Viper one's reply. There was none. His own shield was now at 46%, and he was getting alarms from the Starcraft computer. If he didn't correct his reentry angle immediately, he would be as doomed as his wingman.

Leave him. The thought rose up from some dark corner of his mind. He rejected it and pushed steeper still.

He's a Colloquial...you're an Elite...royalty in fact...leave him! The unknown voice rose again, causing Daeson to hesitate.

"Viper three, maintain proper reentry parameters," came Viper one's command to Daeson.

His wingman slipped further below him, and he fought to push steeper, but his hand would not comply.

"Viper three, maintain proper reentry parameters!" Viper one repeated.

Let him die...your life is worth a hundred of his.

Daeson began pulling back on his stick to recover a safe reentry angle. A battle was warring within him to control his actions. Viper four sunk further below him.

No! Daeson screamed within himself. He clicked his com button.

"Hang on, Tig, I'm coming for you."

Daeson rebelled against logic and the voice that commanded him to leave the condemned wingman. He shoved his control stick forward and screamed downward through the fiery curtain before him.

"Negative, Viper three!" Nawlin ordered. "Cadet Lockridge, resume proper reentry parameters." Daeson knew the instructor was more concerned about his own skin than either of his students'. Losing a member of the royal family to a reentry training mission would mean the end of him.

"Viper four, do you have lateral control?"

"Affirmative, Viper three."

"I'm going to engage my grappling field to the front of your Starcraft to decrease the angle of attack and lessen the reentry vector," Daeson radioed.

"Roger, Viper three. Shield at 14%. Hull temperature 3200°!" His voice was strained.

"Viper three, this is Viper one. Break off from Viper four. Grappling during reentry has never been done before. You'll never get close enough to affect a lock."

Daeson ignored the instructor and concentrated on the sequence of his next actions. He knew he had less than thirty seconds, and maneuvering close enough to engage his grappling field during the extreme buffeting of a steep reentry would be nearly impossible. What he was about to attempt was beyond foolish, but he could not idly watch as a fellow pilot plummeted to certain fiery death, even if Tig was a Colloquial. The radio now remained silent.

Against the bellowing complaints of his Starcraft's computer voice, Daeson forced his vessel steeper still. The cockpit was becoming uncomfortably hot. The controls were sluggish, so he adapted. Fifteen seconds....now just forty yards ahead and slightly above Viper three's Starcraft, Daeson targeted the nose of Tig's craft. Ten seconds...he touched the screen to activate the grappler field, and his ship moaned its defiance. His own shield dropped from 32% to 19% instantly as he felt the pull from Viper three's ship.

"You've got me, Viper three!" It was the first hint of hope in the fellow cadet's voice.

Daeson pitched his Starcraft upward and engaged the main thrusters to change their reentry vector. At first there was no effect.

"Shield failure imminent!" Viper four's voice resumed its strained plea.

Daeson's shield was now at 12%, and the glow on his cockpit canopy nearly obliterated everything from his view. He increased power to his thrusters, straining the Starcraft's structure beyond its limits. Then agonizingly slow, the tandem Starcrafts' entry vectors began to lift.

"Come on," Daeson whispered. "Pull up."

At first, the angle changed by fractions of a degree, but the strategy was working. Daeson had to make perfectly timed corrections to the controls as he coerced the Starcrafts upward. He forced his muscles to relax so he could feel the ship and properly control it. He kept a close eye on his own hull temperature, as that would be his first indication of a true reversal of impending calamity. He deftly maneuvered and enticed his Starcraft until their reentry vector was nearly back to normal.

"It's working, Viper three!" Tig's voice was enthusiastic. "Hull temperature is dropping, and my E-shield strength is increasing!"

After a few more moments of careful maneuvering, the transition from space to atmospheric flight was complete. Daeson had to maintain a grappler lock on Tig's Starcraft all the way to the landing pad. Once their forward velocity was zero and the horizontal stabilizer was not needed, Daeson released the lock so that Tig could descend the last hundred feet to the tarmac. Daeson took a deep breath and carefully maneuvered his own Starcraft through the massive hanger doors and into its designated bay. He could tell that the brutal re-entry had damaged his own Starcraft to some degree.

By the time he climbed down the cockpit ladder, he had an audience—emergency personnel, the maintenance crew, his flight mates, and of course his instructor. Nawlin was the first he would have to face. His face was hot with anger. Daeson stole a quick glance at Xandra over Nawlin's shoulder. He couldn't quite read her...those fierce eyes and a slight smile. She was both angry and impressed.

"Cadet Lockridge, you put yourself and your Starcraft at grave risk! You disobeyed an order from your instructor and jeopardized the life of a fellow cadet!" The instructor's nostrils flared, and his jaw muscles clenched, but Daeson knew that the full fury of the instructor's anger would not be unleashed on him for the simple fact that he was of the royal family.

"My fellow cadet's life was already in jeopardy...sir." Daeson stared back at the instructor. Rarely did Daeson attempt to take advantage of his Royal status, but under these circumstances, he couldn't stop himself.

The instructor glared back. "Be prepared to answer to the Academy Commander for your actions today!" Then he glanced at the other two students. "Debrief in thirty minutes!" Swinging his gear bag over his shoulder, he pushed past them toward the squadron quarters.

Once he was out of earshot, Daeson looked at Xandra and Tig with a raised eyebrow. "Is it me, or does he seem a little upset?"

Neither laughed.

"That was pretty stupid," Xandra said with clenched teeth. Daeson still wasn't sure if she wanted to hit him or hug him. Tig interrupted.

"Master Lockridge, I don't know how to thank you. What you did up there for me...I..."

"It would've been a shame to see a Starcraft burn up like that," Daeson cut him off and winked. "Let's get something to drink before we get to enjoy this debrief, shall we?" Tig nodded, and Daeson led the three of them toward the squadron. Silently Daeson was plagued by thoughts of how hard it had been to convince himself to try to save Tig. He certainly didn't feel like the hero that Tig thought him to be.

"Cadets Lockridge and Tigratinna." The voice came from near his Starcraft. The three cadets turned.

A maintenance chief was performing an initial inspection on Daeson's Starcraft. A young female mechanic technician or "mechtech" was standing beside the chief, preoccupied with her own inspection of Daeson's Starcraft. Daeson had seen her many times before since the schedule usually designated one of two Starcrafts for him to fly—hers being one of them. Both the chief and the mechtech wore faces of mild disdain, but since they were both Drudges, Daeson wasn't too concerned about their additional chastisement.

The chief turned his full attention to Daeson. "We need to have a maintenance debrief with you so we can effect repairs as soon as possible...sir."

Daeson noticed the female mechtech was still mesmerized by the scoring on the leading edges of the Starcraft.

"It'll have to wait until after—"

"What in Omega were you doing up there to cause this kind of damage?" the mechtech asked without looking up, shaking her head in confusion.

Xandra snarled, "Watch your tongue, Drudge! You're speaking to Master Lockridge of the royal family!"

At that the girl stopped her inspection and glared at Xandra, taking two steps forward to stand beside the chief. She crossed her arms, fire burning in her eyes.

"This Starcraft was..."

"We can wait until after your debrief with the squadron," the chief interrupted. He held a gentle hand in front of the mechtech. "That will give us time to download the flight data from the computer and begin a structural analysis."

Xandra looked as if she were about to tear into the girl. The mechtech seemed to realize her folly and lowered her gaze. She stepped back with clenched fists at her side.

Daeson nodded to the chief then took a moment to stare at the girl. She was obviously trying to avoid his eyes, but it seemed impossible. She finally glanced up, and Daeson continued to stare at her until she averted her eyes again. He was testing her. She was gutsy for a Drudge. Of average height, her stature did nothing to diminish the bold spirit within her. Daeson held his gaze a little longer—a silent show of authority. After two more seconds of silent lashings, he was about to turn his back, but the girl rebelled and lifted her eyes once more to his.

No timidity was evident in her gaze but rather a bold countenance of defiance. Dark hair framed her dark brown eyes, which revealed a stare that pushed back against twelve hundred years of subjugation. Daeson felt his anger rise, yet something about her response pleased him. He had never really noticed her before...a silent cog in the background, keeping the Jyptonian way of life functioning smoothly. But for a moment, she transcended from servant to a vibrant, living being with personality, moxie, and a rugged beauty.

"That will work, chief," Daeson replied. "The debrief may go a little long, but we'll be back right after."

"Thank you, sir," the chief replied.

The female mechtech and Daeson were still locked in a millennial dual when the chief grabbed her shoulder and spun her about, back toward the Starcraft.

"We're not Drudge. We're Raylean!" Daeson and his flight-mates heard the girl whisper to the chief.

"The insolence!" Xandra exclaimed.

Daeson thought she might take out after the young mechtech, so he grabbed Xandra's arm and pulled her along toward the pilot lounge, motioning for Tig to follow.

"She should be released and sent to work cleaning reactor cores for the power grid," Xandra shouted over her shoulder toward the retreating chief and his mechtech.

"Yes," Daeson said. "Probably...but not today."

The flight debrief went as expected. Daeson was required to repeat the mission as a corrective action. Then Daeson and Tig met with the maintenance chief to explain in detail what had happened so the two Starcrafts could be effectively repaired. The female mechtech was noticeably absent.

As a result of Daeson's meetings, he was late to the midday meal. He collected his food from the replicator and joined Linden, Xandra, and another friend, Brehan, at their table. Linden lifted an eyebrow as he sat down, but Daeson just shook his head as he started quickly shoveling food in his mouth. He was sure Linden had already heard about the morning's events from Xandra. He glanced up only briefly at Linden and then to Xandra. In spite of his efforts, Daeson sensed his relationship with Linden was waning, and he wondered if it had to do with Xandra or his competitive standing in the academy for top cadet. Whatever the reason, it seemed that the rift had been accentuated when Linden started his royalty government training to become Chancellor of Jypton with his father and the other Elite men of power two years ago.

Daeson was left to finish up his meal by himself and then rushed to make Talon training with the rest of his class. He donned his black body armor and entered the training arena just as the cadets were called to attention, fastening the last of his bootstraps and jumping in line a moment later.

The Talon instructor was an experienced Elite pilot of twenty-two years. A prime specimen of decades of rigorous conditioning, countless hours of advanced weapons training, and a daily regimen of Deitum Prime supplement, Aero Force Master Broadwick commanded the respect of every cadet. To Broadwick it didn't matter if the cadets were Royal, Elite, or Colloquial: he was here to do one job, and he did it well.

"It looks like we have our first volunteer for combat demo this afternoon." Broadwick walked slowly toward Daeson.

Daeson cringed. This would be painful, and he was already sore from yesterday's abrupt meeting with the ground.

"Cadet Daeson, front and center," Broadwick barked.

Daeson stepped forward, executed a square corner, and presented himself before the instructor with a salute.

"Why are you late to Talon training, cadet?" Broadwick demanded.

Daeson eyed Broadwick. The entire academy would have heard about the incident of the morning by now. Nearly losing two Starcraft was no small emergency.

"I have no excuse, sir," Daeson replied.

Broadwick squinted at Daeson.

"That's what I thought. Prepare for combat!"

Daeson drew his Talon from the holster, extended the black steel blade, and assumed a combat stance. He felt the power of the Talon coursing in his hands, anxious to be wielded.

The Talon was a handheld weapon of elegance and power. Like the architecture of Jypton, this gleaming instrument had a history that melded the ancient with the modern. Centuries earlier, a brilliant weaponeer named Cheed Talon, a descendant from the people of the planet Mesos, had discovered a way to assemble and disassemble a metallic composite at the molecular level, using a powerful stasis field to maintain shape integrity. He had been able to design a weapon that would extend and shape the metallic composite into a blade of various lengths, from knife to full-length sword. The stasis field not only maintained the strength and integrity of the metal when applied, but it also served as a cutting edge with unparalleled sharpness.

Years later Cheed implemented the addition of a plasma energy discharge module to the Talon that could be fired at will once the composite blade was retracted.

The most useful modification Cheed adopted late in his life was the nearly instantaneous conversion from blade to discharge weapon. The addition of the mode selector allowed the operator to hold the Talon as a sword or knife, and with the press of the selector, the blade would retract, causing the stasis generator to tilt to the perfect angle of a hand-held energy weapon, allowing for much more accurate aiming and firing. This made the Talon a perfect solution for each combat situation and solved the issue of needing to carry multiple cumbersome weapons. Over the following few hundred years, subtle improvements had been made, but Cheed Talon's original design seemed timeless. He was a man a millennium ahead of his time.

Instructor Broadwick circled Daeson and evaluated his stance before the cadets, making slight adjustments in foot position. He then demonstrated a new move that took advantage of the Talon's variable blade extension capability when transitioning from close combat to hand-to-hand. After using Daeson to demonstrate, Broadwick scanned the rest of the cadets.

THE TALON

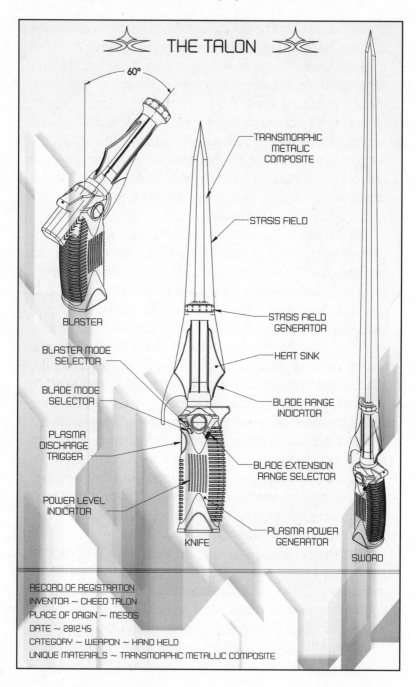

60°

TRANSMORPHIC
METALLIC
COMPOSITE

STASIS FIELD

STASIS FIELD
GENERATOR

HEAT SINK

BLADE RANGE
INDICATOR

BLADE EXTENSION
RANGE SELECTOR

PLASMA POWER
GENERATOR

BLASTER

BLASTER MODE
SELECTOR

BLADE MODE
SELECTOR

PLASMA
DISCHARGE
TRIGGER

POWER LEVEL
INDICATOR

KNIFE

SWORD

RECORD OF REGISTRATION
INVENTOR ~ CHEED TALON
PLACE OF ORIGIN ~ MESOS
DATE ~ 2812.45
CATEGORY ~ WEAPON ~ HAND HELD
UNIQUE MATERIALS ~ TRANSMORPHIC METALLIC COMPOSITE

"Who would like to volunteer to fight cadet Lockridge?"

At first no one moved. Then three hands rose, but it was Linden who stepped forward.

"I will."

Daeson looked at Linden, and although there seemed to be a pleasant smile on his face, Daeson could see a simmering anger deep in his eyes. Obviously Daeson's rescue of Xandra, as well as her retelling of his reentry from this morning, was indeed affecting the balance of their trio. Knowing that Xandra had probably been drawn even closer to Daeson as a result of his daring rescue didn't set well with the future chancellor of Jypton, and this was an arena in which Linden was truly a master.

Broadwick smiled. "Very good...Lockridge vs. Lockridge. We'll simulate close combat with power modules exhausted. Make sure your stasis field and plasma discharge safeties are on so there is no body armor penetration."

Daeson verified his safeties were on and locked. Linden did the same. They faced off and nodded to one another. Broadwick signaled for them to engage, and the fight was on. Linden came at Daeson with an aggressive sequence of cuts and slices. Daeson deflected each then countered. His mind flashed back to when they were boys practicing in the courtyard of the palace. They had the advantage over every other cadet because of the advance training with the Talon they had received early on. Once in a great while, Daeson won, but Linden was usually the victor. This duo would be the most equally matched, but no matter the outcome, Daeson feared that the wedge between them would only be driven deeper.

As the advances and counters continued, so did the intensity of the fight, and Broadwick let it go. Daeson couldn't stop fully committing to the fight, and neither could Linden. Within a couple of minutes, the sparring exercise escalated to an all-out war. The other students watched in stunned silence as Linden and Daeson unleashed their aggression on each other.

Daeson finally saw a moment of weakness in Linden and took advantage of it. He thwarted a thrust by Linden, spun inward toward him while retracting his blade to knife-length for a plunge to Linden's chest, the exact move Broadwick and just taught them. But Linden was ready for it. Linden's free arm diverted the thrust and executed a short blade plunged toward Daeson's heart. The maneuver frightened Daeson, for even with the stasis field off, the power of the thrust could potentially penetrate his breast armor. At the last second, Linden stopped, the tip of his blade indenting the outer surface of Daeson's armor. Face to face, Daeson felt something dark and heavy in Linden's penetrating eyes.

"I yield," Daeson said quietly to his friend.

Slowly, Linden's eyes softened, and he felt the knife retreat. Both men were breathing heavily.

"Well fought, my lord," Daeson took a step back and bowed.

Linden nodded. There seemed a subtle look of regret on his face. He straightened his shoulders.

"And you, Cadet Lockridge."

Broadwick approached them.

"That final move was poorly timed, Cadet Lockridge," he said, looking at Daeson.

Daeson nodded his acceptance of the criticism, but the instructor's gaze lingered.

"Pair up," Broadwick called out. "Check safeties on and begin sparring. I want to see every move that I have taught you in the past two weeks being practiced. Engage!"

After Talon practice, Daeson showered and exited the arena complex with Linden, Xandra, and Brehan.

"Great match today," Daeson acknowledged, glancing over at his cousin.

Linden eyed Daeson. "You too."

Though the facade of friendship was somewhat restored, something had shifted—permanently; Daeson could feel it. Evidently Xandra could too.

"How about we catch some food off campus later?" Xandra offered.

"I'm game," Brehan replied.

Brehan was an Elite from a powerful family, much like Xandra. As Daeson's relationship with Linden had strained, Daeson had come to appreciate Brehan more and more. He was a bit shorter than Daeson but as strong as a Kolazo beast and loyal as the day was long.

"Sounds good," Daeson added. "I'll catch up with you later." He swung his towel around his neck. "I have to give the maintenance chief a few more details on the flight this morning."

Xandra looked as if she were going to offer to accompany him, but there wasn't a reason strong enough to justify it, so Daeson gave a subtle shake of his head. She flashed him a quick smile and resumed her walk with Linden and Brehan.

Daeson couldn't help wondering what was happening with Linden. He had changed or rather was changing. The sober look of power was in his countenance. It was the same look that his father, Chancellor Marcus Lockridge, conveyed. Was it simply the weight of responsibility that had lowered his brow, or was there something more?

CHAPTER

3

Raviel

Artificial Intelligence Wars—a century-long period of wars between humans and androids endowed with artificial intelligence or AI. The first war began on the planet of Mesos and spread quickly throughout the galaxy, costing countless lives and destroying the livelihoods of many planets.

D aeson walked toward the chief's office, then glanced to his left. He diverted to the hangar instead. The day was nearly spent, and the academy was quickly being emptied of its personnel as Daeson entered the hanger, stepping up to the rail that overlooked this beautiful array of space steeds below him. He felt something deep inside him shiver. It was almost as if he were entering hallowed ground. The sight of thirty T32 Starcrafts bathing in the soft light of this massive hangar stirred his soul. These T32's were trainers, but all they were missing to be quickly transformed into the deadly A32 attack Starcrafts was a full complement of energy weapons. This phase of Daeson's training would begin within the next couple of weeks, and he couldn't wait!

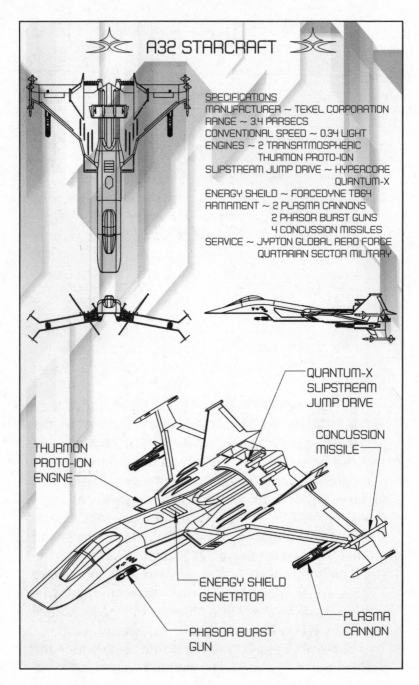

A32 STARCRAFT

SPECIFICATIONS
MANUFACTURER ~ TEKEL CORPORATION
RANGE ~ 3.4 PARSECS
CONVENTIONAL SPEED ~ 0.34 LIGHT
ENGINES ~ 2 TRANSATMOSPHERIC
        THURMON PROTO-ION
SLIPSTREAM JUMP DRIVE ~ HYPERCORE
                QUANTUM-X
ENERGY SHEILD ~ FORCEDYNE TB64
ARMAMENT ~ 2 PLASMA CANNONS
        2 PHASOR BURST GUNS
        4 CONCUSSION MISSILES
SERVICE ~ JYPTON GLOBAL AERO FORCE
        QUATARIAN SECTOR MILITARY

QUANTUM-X
SLIPSTREAM
JUMP DRIVE

CONCUSSION
MISSILE

THURMON
PROTO-ION
ENGINE

ENERGY SHIELD
GENETATOR

PHASOR BURST
GUN

PLASMA
CANNON

As he took a moment to gaze in reverent reflection and be grateful for his good fortune, his mind turned back to the rescue of Tig earlier that day. His thoughts during the emergency disturbed him. Was it fear that had fought for control of the moment? He hated the idea that he might hesitate at a time when the slightest delay could kill. Such thoughts had seemed foreign to him, and they didn't feel like fear. As a boy he'd had impulses and reactions that had influenced him, but never before had such concise thoughts penetrated his mind. The other emotion that surprised him was how good it felt to do the right thing and complete the rescue, even if Tig was just a Colloquial.

The hangar's cathedral silence was interrupted by the occasional whir of a power wrench. Descending the walkway steps and heading in the direction of the sound of the wrench, he realized he was approaching the Starcraft he had flown earlier that day. Many of the panels had already been removed, with various maintenance carts positioned about the Starcraft's periphery. On the far side, a mechtech was half buried in the underbelly of the machine. Daeson circled the craft, sidestepping tools and panels until he was just beneath the mechtech.

"Will it fly again?" Daeson asked.

The mechtech jolted, dropping a fusion wrench while letting out a yelp followed by a string of words Daeson couldn't quite catch. By the tone, he could tell the mechtech was a female.

Daeson winced before reaching for the wrench at his feet as the mechtech extracted herself from the Starcraft. She dropped to the ground with her back to Daeson. "Don't ever sneak up on a mechtech like that!"

Daeson stood up, and the mechtech turned about. It was the same mechtech that had sassed him earlier that morning with the same fire in her eyes. There was a small cut over her right eye with fresh blood trickling down her temple. Her eyes widened once she recognized Daeson.

"Oh...sorry. Didn't mean to startle you," Daeson said. He couldn't take his eyes off the trickle of blood that was now near her cheek, passing between two grease smudges. The mechtech stared at him in silence for a moment and then lowered her eyes.

"Master Lockridge, I owe you an apology for my words this morning. Please forgive me." She glanced up at him briefly before lowering her gaze again.

Daeson hadn't expected that. He glanced at her nametag.

"I did a number on your Starcraft, Mechtech Arko. What's the rest of your name?"

She looked at him rather bewildered. "I am...Raviel."

"Tell me, was that a real apology, or do you just want to keep your job?"

Fear flashed across Raviel's face, and Daeson realized that his tease wasn't fair. He was toying with her life. He rarely considered the plight of those in the Drudge caste, for their position was simply a part of the culture...a faceless workforce at the disposal of the Jyptonians. He grinned, but her eyes furrowed.

"I want to keep my job."

Daeson nodded and smiled again. "That's what I thought. Are you good at it?"

Slowly the lines of tension eased on her face. She actually smiled, and it set him back. Her eyes lit up, and it was as if he were looking at a completely different person.

"Why do you think they assign you to my Starcraft?"

Daeson raised an eyebrow. He hated being coddled, and it hadn't crossed his mind that even the mechtechs assigned to his Starcraft might be part of his protection.

"Then I guess I'll just have to accept your apology. Can't lose a good mechtech."

Raviel smiled again and looked relieved. By now the trickle of blood was nearly to her chin. Daeson handed her his towel.

"You have a little blood on your cheek there," he added, pointing to the right side of her face.

She reached up and touched her temple. When she saw the blood on her fingers, she accepted the towel and wiped the blood away. Daeson pointed to her chin and she wiped some more.

"I heard what you did to save that other pilot. I was...," she hesitated.

"Impressed?" Daeson finished.

"Surprised," Raviel corrected as she handed the towel back.

"Oh." Her comment stung.

"Sorry about your towel," Raviel said sheepishly.

"Sorry about your head," Daeson said with a grin. "How long have you been a mechtech?"

"Nearly three years."

"You started young," Daeson replied.

"I had to. My family needed the income."

Daeson realized that he never had to think about income. He and she lived in two different worlds.

"Do you work this late every night?" Daeson glanced about the hangar. "Looks like you're one of the few left."

"My Starcraft has the record for fewest down days...or at least it did." Raviel lifted an accusing eyebrow.

"Ah...so now I'm guilty for making you work late and tarnishing your perfect record too."

Raviel shrugged and nodded. Daeson recognized that he was close to being guilty of fraternization, but something about this girl tugged on him. He scanned the hangar to see if anyone had noticed them yet. For an Elite, not to mention a Royal, to have a casual conversation with a Drudge was unthinkable.

Raviel apparently noticed Daeson's uneasiness.

"Well, I'd better get back to my repairs. Somebody really broke this thing." Raviel flashed Daeson another smile and then held out her hand. Her smile had refreshed that same odd response inside him, and he looked at her outstretched hand, confused. To touch a Drudge was an appalling breach in cultural etiquette. What was she doing?

"Can I have my wrench back?" Raviel asked.

Daeson looked down and realized he was still holding it.

"Oh...of course," he answered as he handed her the wrench.

She grabbed it and spun around, returning to her work platform. She deftly hoisted herself back onto the platform and began working her way up into the Starcraft's underbelly.

"Good luck with the repairs," he called up to her.

"Better luck with the flying," she called down, stealing a glance beneath the arm stretched above her head.

Daeson laughed, but this time the look from this lowly mechtech rattled his heart in a way that surprised him. He shook his head and walked away, trying to forget that glance but not really wanting to. *What was that?* He wondered. Her eyes...something about her eyes.

Raviel watched Lockridge turn around and walk away. A scowl slowly replaced the pleasant countenance she had worn just seconds earlier. She loathed Lockridge and everything about him...what he stood for...what he meant to her people. Painful memories swept over her before she could stop them: memories of her older sister, Aliza, lying in a pool of blood on the street outside their home, her mother and father weeping, and cold, heartless sentries walking on as if the mayhem of their unjustified assault was of no consequence.

Aliza had been accused of subversion of the Jyptonian government. Raviel never knew if Aliza had indeed been associated with some sort of resistance movement within the Raylean people, but on that sorrowful night six years ago, Raviel had sworn that whatever it was that Aliza was accused of, she would be a part of it. Her sister's death had crafted within her a heart of blazing bitterness that would be quieted by nothing less than rebellion against the Jyptonians.

Raviel took a breath to quell her rising anger and then took a moment to analyze what had just happened. She had a subtle sense that the Royal's interest was more than just the status of repairs of the Starcraft. She wondered if his seeming interest could be used to their advantage somehow. If he came back, she would know for sure. The next time she met with the council, she would mention it and let them decide.

The Plexus had recruited her when she was young, shortly after Aliza's death. Her aptitude for aerotech had been evident early on, and her residency in the capital city of Athlone was exactly what they were looking for. Using other Raylean agents inside the academy, they had been able to position her as the lead mechtech on Daeson Lockridge's Starcraft. The goal had been Linden Lockridge, but the council seemed content with his cousin as an alternative.

Raviel still wasn't sure what the Plexus Council's intent was, but her mission was to gain as much information about the Lockridge family as possible, especially the prince and his cousin—training levels, daily routines, entertainment habits, hobbies, personality characteristics. As a mechtech this would be difficult, but she also knew that she was just a small piece of the intelligence gathering effort. The brilliant minds behind the Plexus would compile a profile that would one day allow them an "opportunity."

She was compartmentalized, not knowing what the grand plan was or what the "opportunity" might eventually be. Was it subterfuge, revolt, or perhaps even escape? Raviel shook her head at the thought. It seemed so impossible. How could a race of people so oppressed ever hope to effect any significant change against an empire as strong as the Jyptonians? But Raviel played her part well, motivated by the pain of a wounded past. Besides this, she really did love the tech that allowed fantastic machines to fly. Working on the Starcraft had been her dream, and she was good at her job. But her most earnest dream would never be realized—flying one. Rayleans were forbidden from flight within any craft that could escape Jypton's atmosphere.

Raviel touched her head where she had earlier wiped away the blood. It was tender. Lockridge actually seemed to care, which angered and frustrated her at the same time. She didn't want him to be anything but the rude and heartless monster she had conjured up for him and the rest of the royal family to be. She replayed their exchange, annoyed by the subtle tug in her gut that told her he might be different. She clenched her teeth and reminded herself that all Elite were oppressive, dictatorial, heartless overlords and responsible for the deaths of countless fellow Rayleans. If the Plexus asked her to *encourage* Lockridge's apparent interest, she would have to play her part in a way she had never imagined. She steeled herself for the task before her.

That evening Daeson, Linden, Xandra and Brehan met at their favorite club for food and fun. They had the next three days off from the academy, so Daeson had told his mother not to expect him to be home. Daeson was now forced to give a detailed account of the morning's flight to his friends.

"I can't believe you risked your life to save a Colloquial." Linden was shaking his head. "This is exactly why my father almost didn't let us into the academy in the first place." He had to speak slightly louder than usual to overcome the music emanating from the adjoining dance hall.

Linden was relaxed, almost back to his old self. The club atmosphere seemed to have erased whatever it was that was affecting him...at least for a while.

Daeson spotted the two royal guards dressed in casuals three tables to his left. They would be here for Linden. The prince was never unprotected. A hovering service bot delivered four drinks to their table while they waited for their food. After the Galactic AI Wars eight hundred and fifty years earlier, no service robot could emulate human personality in any way, and programming code restrictions were unilaterally agreed upon throughout the galaxy.

"I have to agree, Daeson," Brehan piped in. "You can't take those risks, or they'll eliminate you from training. In fact, I can't believe they haven't already pulled the plug on you."

"I'm sure they would have if Linden hadn't intervened," Daeson said before taking a long drink.

Brehan looked at Linden. "Really?"

"I promised my father that Daeson would never do such a foolish thing again!" Linden glared at Daeson, looking genuinely perturbed. "You're going to get us both eliminated."

"It *was* foolish," Xandra piped in. "And spectacular! Even though the instructor was angry, I could tell he was impressed." Her eyes beamed with pride. "Kinda making this a habit, aren't you?"

"What?" Brehan asked.

Linden and Daeson both stared daggers at her. Their wing suit jumping had to stay a secret.

"Do something like that again, and we'll kill you ourselves!" Xandra said, catching the hint.

Daeson shook his head in apparent disgust. "Here we are at our favorite club with three days off to relax, and you three want to spend it chastising me for demonstrating my outstanding piloting skills?" Daeson let a wide grin spread across his face.

Just then two cadets entered the club, and Daeson immediately recognized one of them. The others at the table caught his stare and followed his eyes. Everyone hushed as Tig, the pilot Daeson had saved earlier, approached them—something unthinkable for a Colloquial in a public recreational setting. Linden's royal guards watched closely as Tig carefully walked toward Daeson.

Daeson glanced around the table and noticed the disdain on the faces of his friends. They would consider such fraternization an embarrassment, especially with Linden present.

Tig stopped a few feet away.

"Please forgive the interruption, Master Lockridge." He quickly glanced toward Linden. "Prince Lockridge," Tig added with a head bow.

"What is it, Tig?" Daeson questioned, with a slight grin forming to ease the tension as he turned in his chair to face Tig more directly.

Tig hesitated, glancing once more at Daeson's companions and then back to him before he spoke. "I don't know why you risked your life to save me today, Master Lockridge, but I want you to know that I am indebted to you." At that, Tig's countenance hardened to serious resolve.

A pithy reply would only dishonor Tig's allegiant words, so Daeson said nothing.

"If ever you need anything—anything—I'm an ally forever." Tig didn't wait for a reply; he simply bowed his head and turned away.

Daeson wasn't sure what to do next, so he sat with his back to his friends for a few seconds longer.

"Ally?" Linden said, breaking the awkward silence. "Sounds like you're going to war."

They all laughed as Daeson turned to rejoin them. He flashed them a condescending smile. "Yeah...yeah. What were we talking about?"

"You and your foolish risks." Brehan shot a side-glance toward the retreating Colloquial cadet.

"Oh, yes," Daeson said, pointing at each of them. "And none of you have ever done anything risky...like Banshi-beast riding, hover racing, or dodging magnetic fire geysers on your aerobikes?"

Linden and Brehan looked at each other. "Dodging magnetic fire geysers?" Linden asked.

Daeson eyed Xandra accusingly.

"Seriously?" Brehan asked.

Xandra shrugged. "It's quite a thrill. You should try it."

Brehan smiled wide. "Let's go!"

Daeson, Linden, and Xandra shared a knowing look.

As the day wore on, Daeson's muscles had grown quite sore. "Maybe next time…I've had enough thrill for a while," he responded. Linden agreed, and Xandra actually looked relieved.

CHAPTER

4

When Worlds Collide

Aerobike – A single or two-person transportation or security vehicle utilizing a grav-tech engine for vertical hover suspension. Horizontal thrust is attained by a variety of propulsion drives, the most typical being the betatron turbine.

Daeson thoroughly enjoyed the time off with his friends and avoided most of the potentially awkward situations with Xandra and Linden. Daeson wished Xandra would just give up on him and allow Linden into her life, but a deeper part of him hoped for something different. He couldn't deny it...there was a lot to like about Xandra—smart, beautiful, athletic, and full of adventure. If Linden would just set his eyes on another girl, the problem would disappear. But it seemed as though that was not to be, and he knew that Linden would never back away from a victory he could force if need be.

Daeson and Linden had to return to the palace early to attend a banquet on their last day of leave. Daeson hated such events, but Linden thrived on them.

"You were born for this sort of thing," Daeson said as he and Linden walked side by side to the opulent banquet hall. They were dressed in the pristine formal academy uniform, and though their rank markings signified them as cadets, the distinctly royal festoons signified power and respect.

They stopped briefly on the elevated walkway that gave them a fabulous view of the palace spaceport. An elegant transport ship was just now extending its landing struts. The red and black emblem was unmistakable.

"Don't look so glum, Daeson," Linden said with an air of authority. "Tonight we will meet Chancellor Treville himself, leader of the Galactic Alliance."

Daeson looked over at his cousin.

"And this excites you?"

Linden glared at Daeson, motioning for him to follow on toward the banquet hall.

"Next to my father, Treville is the most powerful man in the galaxy. Yes, this excites me, and it should you too."

Linden lifted his chin as they prepared to enter the hall.

The Galactic Alliance was an unusual amalgam of planets that appeared unified only by Chancellor Treville's leadership, for there seemed to be no consistent unifying cause, at least to Daeson. At times, members of the Alliance were even at war with each other, but Treville was always present to offer counsel and arbitration when needed. His resources seemed limitless and his power far reaching. Ultimately, the

Alliance also played a key role in ensuring the galaxy-wide distribution of Deitum Prime.

Daeson took a deep breath, straightened his back, pulled back his shoulders, and entered alongside Linden. The young men were first greeted by Daeson's mother: proper, cool, and calculated. But underneath her calm exterior, Daeson could see her swelling heart and subtle smile. Daeson tried to defer the many introductions and conversations to Linden when at all possible. The mild hum of the hall diminished to silence when the arrival of Chancellor Zari Treville was announced.

Treville entered the hall with two courtiers by his side. To Daeson's surprise, the Chancellor did not strut or put on airs...he didn't need to. A power emanated from his being, and everyone in the hall knew it, including Chancellor Lockridge. In the court of the Royals, the smallest and subtlest of actions tell all.

Lockridge briefly lowered his gaze ever so slightly then looked back to Treville's eyes, while Treville's gaze was as steady as Jypton's sun. Offering a careful smile, Lockridge tilted his head a few degrees. Treville did not smile but nodded his response. Lockridge then lifted an arm to guide Treville to his first introduction, but Treville hesitated before stepping forward.

As Daeson watched Linden's father greet the Chancellor, he wondered at Linden's words. *Second* to his father? He thought not. Even though Jypton was by far the most powerful planet in the galaxy and the Alliance was supposed to be more of an association than an authority, the interaction between these two men said otherwise. After introductions to other Royals and highly positioned Elite, Linden brought Daeson to meet the Chancellor, and Linden was nervous. Linden was never nervous—about anything.

This made Daeson all the more anxious about meeting Treville.

"Chancellor Treville, please meet my cousin and fellow academy cadet, Daeson Lockridge."

When Treville set his eyes on Daeson, Daeson's heart quickened. He had heard once that the eyes of a man were the windows to his soul. If this were true, Daeson felt as if he were gazing into the soul of more than a mortal man, and he instantly understood the respect Treville commanded. But there was something more here—something frightening.

"Young Daeson Lockridge," Treville offered his welcome. His hand was warm and familiar, yet dark, as if Daeson were shaking hands with the architect of all of his nightmares. He felt lured, overpowered, and insignificant. Did everyone feel this way in Treville's presence?

"Chancellor Treville," Daeson said with a slight bow, "I am honored to meet you."

"And I you, Cadet Lockridge."

His discomfort growing by the moment, Daeson tried to release, anxious to move on quickly now that the formality of the introduction was finished, but Treville held on to Daeson's hand. The strength of it was intimidating.

"I am told you are performing near the top of your academy class," Treville said with a penetrating gaze.

"Training has gone well, sir."

The Chancellor put his free hand on Daeson's right shoulder and pulled him closer. Daeson felt his cheeks flush, sweat threatening to bead. "You have great promise as a future leader on Jypton," Treville said, his voice deep and quiet. "Be wary of false beginnings— they will destroy you."

Like ashes from a fire, Treville's words floated in through his ears and rested on the pedestal of his soul. The moment hung suspended until Treville released his grip on Daeson's hand and shoulder and turned to the next Elite. Daeson slowly stepped back and away from the man. Without understanding what had just happened, he felt conquered and exposed. He wanted to be away, away from these people and this man.

Daeson endured the meal and the casual conversations but never once more dared look into the eyes of Chancellor Treville. That night on his bed, Daeson couldn't make the dark words of Chancellor Treville go away. What did he mean? Daeson's sleep was fitful at best that night.

The next day classes and training went well in spite of his unsettled spirit. By the end of the day, everything seemed back to normal, and Daeson found himself walking toward the T32 hanger once again. This time Xandra found him and joined him in his walk.

"Hey...mind if I join you?" she asked, not waiting for an answer. "Where are we going?"

"I'm just checking to see if they've started weaponizing some of the T32's. Can't wait to start our next phase of training."

Xandra smiled. "Me too. Something about a couple of plasma cannons on the wings of a 32 just kills it."

Daeson nodded. "No doubt."

As he glanced over at her, her eyes warmed. "I never have had a chance to properly thank you for saving my life during the jump." She flashed him a smile that seemed different than usual—it was inviting. "I wanted to thank you privately." She looked away, her cheeks slightly flushed. Daeson had never seen Xandra as anything but guarded. This was unusual.

"You and Linden would have done the same for me," Daeson said, trying to stiff-arm words that should not be spoken.

"I had a good time on our days off—with you," she added.

Daeson swallowed hard. Those last two words contained a thousand unspoken thoughts, a flood of bridled emotions, and the potential for a royal scandal of global proportions. He walked in silence until they entered the hangar, staring out over the T32s but not really seeing them. They stood shoulder to shoulder, but Xandra said nothing more. She knew what those words meant. It was Daeson's move. Could he be as daring—or perhaps as foolish—as she?

"I did too," he finally replied. "...have a good time with you."

Xandra turned and looked at him, her eyes conveying the full ache and hope in her heart. When he turned to face her, she grabbed his hand.

"I can't...we can't...," Daeson began, but she leaned closely into him.

"Why not?" she asked, her lips nearly touching his. "Don't you want this for us?"

Daeson hesitated. Conflicted, he took a deep breath and then stepped back. "No, Xandra," he said softly. "I don't want this for us because of what it would mean for you, me, Linden, and all of our families! Our lives would be ruined...the ramifications could last for generations."

When she looked directly at him, her eyes revealed her resentment against the expectations of royal family duty. As she tilted her head, red spiral curls fell across her shoulder. Hurt was evident in her gaze. "I need to know...if we weren't bound by royal obligations, would you be with me?" she asked.

Daeson raised an eyebrow. This one simple question exposed layers of possible outcomes and emotions. He could simply answer no, which would crush Xandra's heart but resolve the entire dilemma in an instant. On the other hand, he desperately wanted to answer yes, which evoked a multitude of thoughts. She was everything he should ever want in a girl, but was she the one? Did he want to answer yes out of a desire to beat Linden at the greatest competition they had ever faced?

A hundred more thoughts raced through his mind as he stared at the beautiful Xandra. Speechless, he stood, trying to determine an answer, but it would not come. And as her eyes softened and her countenance fell, it still was not enough to cause him to speak an answer. He had never seen her so vulnerable...so sad. But her vulnerability only lasted a moment for she had her answer.

"There's someone else then." She lifted her chin slightly as if to defy his rejection.

Daeson hesitated to answer. There was no one else of course, but perhaps letting Xandra think so would be easier for her. He felt wholly inadequate at trying to navigate such a complicated tangle of emotions.

"I see," she acknowledged.

Daeson instantly regretted his silence and wanted to take the risk of love with her, but even now, just seconds later, there was no return.

"Xandra," he said, reaching for her, but she stepped back and held up her hand.

"Don't." Her countenance steeled as she turned to walk away.

Daeson watched until she disappeared through the hangar's exit door. He turned and leaned on the railing overlooking the Starcrafts, motionless, trying to process his feelings, but all he really felt was numb. The moment hung on until a side door opened and the female mechtech named Raviel stepped through. She was carrying a small Starcraft part and walking Daeson's direction. As she passed, Daeson looked for some sort of acknowledgment, but there was none. She just kept walking, as any Drudge would do. Her disregard for his presence stung, and with the emotional turmoil from the last few moments, he was in no mood to let it go. He turned and followed her.

"Mechtech Arko," he called.

She looked over her shoulder, stopped, faced him, and lowered her head.

"Yes, my lord?" Her face was empty of emotion.

He paused, a little confused by her response.

"How are the repairs going on the Starcraft?"

"According to schedule. The structural damage was greater than I anticipated, and every actuator has to be replaced. It looks like my conversion to the A32 is going to be delayed a couple of weeks," Raviel stated flatly, never lifting her eyes to look at him.

"I see," Daeson said.

Something about his encounter with Xandra had left him feeling hollow. He needed to talk with someone...anyone.

"Mind if I see the ship?"

Raviel looked up briefly, annoyance evident in her face.

"This way." She swung her head the direction she had been moving. Her rich, dark hair hung in a braid midway down her back. The mechtech uniform fit her frame well, and Daeson was surprised at how strong she was. Most members of the Drudge caste seemed weak and small.

Raviel briskly walked along the outer rim of the hangar toward her Starcraft's bay. Daeson kept pace.

"When does the conversion happen for the rest of the T32s?" Daeson asked.

"It begins tomorrow."

When they arrived at the Starcraft, Raviel immediately began working on replacing a control surface actuator. Daeson walked around the ship once and came to stand next to her.

"Raviel, right?"

The girl finished tightening a fixture and then glanced around the hangar. Other bays had mechtechs working but all at a distance. She looked Daeson straight in the eye with that alluring look of defiance.

"What are you doing?"

Daeson frowned. The question flustered and angered him. "Not worried about your job anymore?"

"Always—and your talking to me will end it very quickly. Reactor core cleaners don't survive long. It's a death sentence."

Daeson lifted a hand to grab the leading edge of the Starcraft's wing. It was still charred from his reentry mission. Whatever it was that had prompted him to talk to her again had vanished.

"Guess I was just looking to—," he stopped midsentence. Nothing he could say would make sense of what he was doing. Talking to a Drudge about Xandra was foolish and dangerous. It made more sense to talk to a service bot.

"Never mind. Sorry to disturb you. Carry on."

Daeson turned and began walking away.

"Master Lockridge," Raviel called out.

Daeson turned. She bit her lip, seeming to struggle within herself.

"Do you know what's really going on?"

Daeson looked back at her. "Going on?"

Raviel nodded and stepped toward him, her bridled defiant countenance replaced with a look of caution.

"What do you mean...going on?"

Raviel hesitated. "You've been deceived...about everything. The Immortals, Deitum Prime, the Scourge...nothing is as it seems."

"I...I have no idea what you're talking about." This girl was strange...but intriguing. Was she crazy?

Raviel looked deep into his eyes and her shoulders fell slightly. "Forgive me. You seemed different than the other Elite. Never mind me...I'm just talking nonsense." She started to turn back to her work.

"Wait a minute," Daeson said. "What do you mean, 'I've been deceived'?"

Raviel shook her head. "I meant nothing by it. Please...I should be about my work."

As if on cue, a com call on her radio interrupted. "Mechtech Arko, I need those structural specs."

Raviel activated her com switch, "Yes, chief. I'll have them for you right away."

She bowed her head and stepped away.

Daeson stood watching her for a few seconds, confounded by this lowly Drudge girl. He turned and walked slowly up the stairway toward the hangar exit, but his mind was not his own. Disordered thoughts flitted back and forth from Xandra to Raviel and the exchanges he'd had with both. He didn't like it when he wasn't mentally focused. And that in itself added to his mounting frustration. He knew that being at home or studying would only give him opportunity to ponder more pointless musings about his day. He needed activity. On his way to his aerobike, he diverted to the Starcraft simulation building next to the hangar.

"I need to get my mind back on what's important...prepping for the A32," he muttered.

He logged in and signed up for a one-hour A32 simulation training mission. It would count toward one of his requirements, so in spite of the late hour of the day, it was time better spent. At first his flying and weapon employment was rough, and he had to reset the mission twice, but as his mind cleared, he was able to focus on the tasks and fly well. He logged out and felt some of the negative fog lift from his mind. *Xandra will just have to deal with reality, and that Drudge girl and her bizarre comments can easily be forgotten.*

Daeson exited the sim building and walked toward the lot for his aerobike. The sun was low, and since he had missed the evening meal, he looked forward to whatever the palace kitchen would offer at this late hour. The activity at the academy was nearly dormant once more, with only an occasional cadet or staff making their way home or back to the campus quarters. As he approached the intersection of two walkways, his timing was such that he fell in step with another, a Drudge in utility clothing with a small pack slung over the shoulder. His thought was to quicken his pace so as not to be positioned awkwardly next to the Drudge.

"Oh."

The subtle exclamation caused him to glance over and see that he was now walking beside Mechtech Arko. Perfect...avoiding awkward was now impossible. She seemed to feel it too. Speeding up or slowing down so they were just far enough apart not to converse would only add to the awkward atmosphere.

Daeson smiled. "We seem to keep running into each other."

Raviel flashed a sheepish smile, and they walked in silence for a few steps.

"You put in some long days," Daeson finally said.

"I guess so. Looks like you do to," Raviel replied.

More silence. Daeson found his mind drifting to their earlier conversation. Shutting his thoughts down, he reminded himself not to disrupt his peaceful state. Silence was preferred. When he arrived at his aerobike, Raviel pressed onward without a word. He jumped on, entered his start code, and waited for the grav engines to power up and lift the bike from its stand, but instead the display flashed red.

'Power module fault,' it read.

"Great!" he exclaimed. He jumped off and knelt down beside the aerobike to open the module access panel, knowing full well that he hadn't a clue what to look for.

"Would you like me to take a look?"

Daeson looked up. Raviel had returned and was looking over his shoulder.

"You know how to work on these?" he asked.

She tilted her head and smirked.

"I can build a Starcraft from spare parts...I should be able to look at an aerobike and tell you if I can fix it."

"Fair enough. Would you?" Daeson asked. He stood and backed up to let her near the bike.

She immediately set to work. Within a few minutes, she closed the panel and looked up at Daeson. "Try it now."

Daeson got on the bike, entered the start sequence, and heard the grav engine purr to life. He smiled as he looked over at Raviel.

"Amazing! Thanks."

"There's a little known reset sequence for those power modules," she explained, wiping her hands on her hips. "But you'd better get that power module replaced because they don't fault out for no reason."

Daeson nodded. "Will do."

"Guess I'd better get going...need to catch my grav-rail," Raviel said, turning to go.

Daeson glanced at the time stamp on his display.

"You won't make it now," he acknowledged.

Raviel shrugged. "It's okay. I'll catch the next one."

Daeson frowned. "That's no good. I'm not going to be responsible for having you sit at a grav-rail terminal by yourself at night for the next two hours." Daeson wagged his head to the seat behind him. "Jump on and I'll give you a ride."

Raviel shook her head, "I can't do that, Master Lockridge." She began looking nervously around. "After all, don't you think we would look pretty conspicuous?" She motioned toward her utility jump suit.

"Are you telling me that mechtech suit is all you have with you?"

"Well, no but..."

"Go change. I'll wait. It's the least I can do to thank you for not leaving me stranded here."

Raviel opened her mouth to protest.

"It's just a ride," he preempted. "What can that hurt?"

She didn't look convinced. She sighed before hurrying off. A few minutes later she returned in a layered loose-fitting blouse and pants, common clothing for a Drudge but less conspicuous than a mechtech jumpsuit. She cautiously mounted the seat behind Daeson, not daring to touch him.

"It's okay, Arko. You'd better hang on. I've been known to throw a rider."

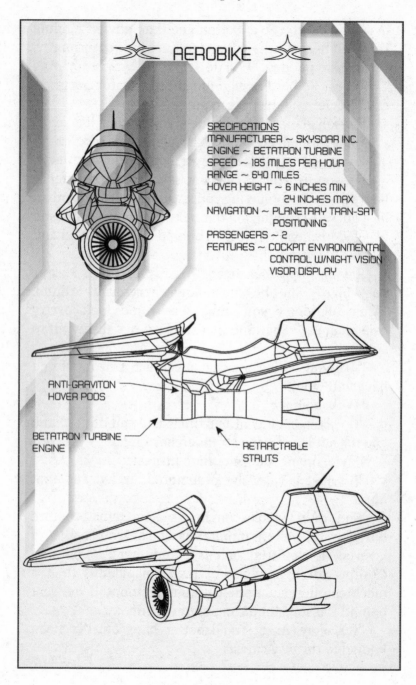

He felt her hands lightly grab the sides of his flight suit. He engaged the grav engine, and they lifted off the stand, which immediately retreated into the underbelly of the aerobike. Accelerating toward the academy gate, Daeson took the less travelled roads. Once off campus, he opened up the throttle and couldn't help pushing it faster than he should have. He felt her grip tighten.

"You can just take me to the next terminal," Raviel said. "I should be able to make that one in time."

"I can just as easily take you home," Daeson replied.

"No! I mean, that won't be necessary," Raviel said. "Please just drop me off at the terminal."

Daeson felt a twinge in his gut. The ordered thoughts he had worked so hard for began to fade, but he didn't seem to mind this time.

"I have a better idea."

He turned off the next exchange and rode south.

"This isn't the way," Raviel said.

"I know. Don't be nervous. We're both hungry, so I'll grab some food for us, and then I'll take you home, okay?"

Raviel didn't reply. After a few more turns, they arrived at an eatery near the ocean walkway.

"Wait here," Daeson ordered. He returned with a bag, jumped back on his aerobike, and rode until they were gliding effortlessly along the sandy shores of the Marricoo Ocean. He accelerated until the cool dusk air made his eyes water. Raviel held on tightly as he veered out over the ocean, skimming the gentle waves. The salty air refreshed him, and he made a wide gentle turn back toward shore, pointing out the luminescent glow from a school of orb fish just beneath the surface. As he leaned into the turn, Raviel reached down and let her fingers skim the surface of the calm waters. He smiled.

After circling the orb fish a couple of times, he brought the aerobike to rest on the banks far from any road or dwelling. Raviel quickly dismounted and looked out toward the ocean, where the glowing orb fish were retreating to the deeper water. Daeson shut down the engine and grabbed the bag of food. As he approached Raviel, she turned and looked at him, her piercing eyes revealing the unspoken question: why am I here? As if to answer, he reached inside the bag and handed a wrapped sandwich to Raviel.

"I heard your stomach while you were working on my aerobike. Thought you should try one of these. Nothing like them anywhere in the galaxy."

"I shouldn't be here...with you," she stated. "Please take me to the terminal."

Daeson couldn't tell if she was angry, afraid, or pleased. The expression she wore seemed to harbor all three emotions.

"I know you're hungry."

She eyed him as she slowly reached for the sandwich.

Daeson chose to ignore the fact that this was a breach of fraternization in every way.

"Sit," he said leading the way.

Raviel sat down, not taking her eyes off of him.

"Please don't be afraid," Daeson said, realizing that she might be questioning his motives. "I'll take you home as soon as we've eaten."

His words seemed to satisfy her. Then he watched as she took a small bite, anticipating her response. Her eyes lit up.

Daeson smiled. "See...nothing like it in the galaxy. I haven't yet figured out what spices they use. But then, maybe I don't want to know," he said with a raised eyebrow.

Raviel tried to squelch a laugh but failed, and it made him happy. As they ate, little was said. The gentle, soothing sound of the waves rumbling onto the shore filled the silence. When he was done with his food, he found himself searching for a delay as Raviel finished her last bite.

"Thank you for the food. That was remarkable." She smiled and looked out toward the ocean. "And I shall never forget the ride over the ocean on an aerobike." She looked back at him with gratitude, in a way that jolted him.

"The real reason I brought you here is to ask you what you meant earlier today when you said I was deceived."

Raviel's smile faded. She looked down at the cream-colored sand and scooped up a handful.

"I'm not so sure I should speak of such things to you, Master Lockridge."

Daeson took a deep breath. "For the next few minutes, I'm not Master Lockridge, okay? I'm just a guy wanting to know what you're thinking."

Raviel seemed mesmerized by the sand as it slowly sifted through her fingers. When it was gone, she looked up to the stars. The final rays of Jypton's sun reflected off her cheeks and eyes. There was something deep about this girl. She wasn't just looking at the stars...she was looking beyond them.

"They're out there, you know...waiting to see what we'll do."

Raviel turned and looked at Daeson, piercing his soul with her eyes....those...those eyes.

"Who's out there?"

"The Immortals," Raviel responded, her eyes searching his for a response.

Daeson considered himself far too intelligent to believe in the fairy tale of the Immortals, but if he were to mock her for such a thing, the conversation would be over.

"You believe them to be real?" he asked, trying to sound sincere.

"More real than you or I."

"Hmm. Have you met one? What do they look like?"

Raviel glanced down. Daeson knew he had hit his mark.

She looked back up at him...undaunted.

"No, I haven't, not that I know of. And if that's your criteria for believing in truth, then most of the galaxy doesn't exist. They look much like you and me."

Daeson couldn't argue with her logic, but it did nothing to convince him.

"What do they want?" he asked.

"The Immortals of Sovereign Ell Yon want to help us. The Immortals of the Torians, or Scourge as we call them, want to rule us." Raviel added no emotion or emphasis. Her comments were simply stated.

"Well, they're not doing a very good job...if they exist. And haven't they had thousands of years to do so?" Daeson retorted, regretting his tone once spoken.

"Actually, the Scourge are winning. They control nearly the entire galaxy."

At that, Daeson nearly laughed. "How can you say that? They don't control me—or Jypton for that matter."

"Are you sure?" Raviel questioned, lifting an eyebrow to emphasize her point. "You can't see it because your mind is clouded with the effects of

Deitum Prime. It has infected every living thing in the galaxy."

Daeson shook his head. "If, as you say, they control most of the galaxy, how do they do it?"

Raviel hesitated. "Don't you see...it's all about mind control. Everything is about mind control. The Deitum Prime this galaxy is so desperate for is the very agent by which the Scourge are influencing and controlling the affairs of mankind. Eventually, they will have so permeated every homeworld with Deitum Prime that there will be no return."

Raviel's enthusiasm was building. She shook her head. "It is assimilating every living thing. Surely you've felt it...that struggle inside you...that battle vying for control of your thoughts and actions."

Daeson knew exactly what she was talking about but had never considered it to be the result of anything other than being human. He remembered his conflicting thoughts about saving Tig...thoughts that didn't seem to be his own.

"That's not the way it's supposed to be," Raviel continued.

Daeson fought the urge to smirk. "How do they control our minds then?" Daeson asked. "Is there some thought-manipulating transmission tower pulsing evil commands into our brains?"

Raviel frowned and looked away. "You mock me," she said quietly, looking back at him. "You asked so I'm telling you."

Daeson lowered his head. "You're right...I'm sorry. I shouldn't have mocked you."

"We don't know how they are transmitting their influences...but it *is* happening."

"Your people...this is why they refuse food and water with Deitum Prime?" Daeson asked, gaining insight into the ways of the Rayleans.

"Yes. Sovereign Ell Yon commanded our forefathers many millennia ago to abstain from it. It's all a lie. Deitum Prime will never bring immortality as everyone thinks. It only brings bondage. The truth is, all who are assimilated by Deitum Prime are they themselves slaves to it and to the Immortals of the Scourge who propound it. Furthermore, it is in fact what robbed humanity of the immortality it once had."

Daeson shook his head again. Now she was messing with the core of his own beliefs.

"That isn't true. Look at what Deitum Prime has done for us," he argued. "Our people are genetically bigger, faster, more enlightened. The results are obvious."

"It's a mirage. The enhanced physical attributes are intended only to carry the lie." She scanned Daeson up and down. "This is not who you really are. Have you ever seen what happens to someone if they try to purge themselves of Deitum Prime?"

Purge themselves? he thought. *Why would anyone ever try such a thing?* He studied Raviel's face, once again intrigued by her and her strange beliefs. Her countenance turned grim as if she remembered a dark secret. She turned away.

"What is it?" Daeson asked. She was disturbed, and it bothered him. He nearly reached for her. *This is strange...what is wrong with me?* he wondered.

"Deitum Prime is why you torment us so," Raviel said. She turned and looked back at him. Ah...there was the anger.

"Torment? Really? We offer your people jobs and opportunity. How can you say such things?" Daeson felt anger rising up within him.

Raviel's eyes narrowed, and she slowly shook her head, as if finding what he had said difficult to believe. "Jobs and opportunity?" her cheeks were flushed, and her voice rose in pitch. "Mining camps on the moons of Tiran and Hobalt that no one ever comes back from? Travel and weapon bans? Sentries that watch our every move, often breaking into our homes without cause? Population control procedures that have murdered millions of our people?"

Raviel jumped up, and Daeson stood with her. The fury in her eyes surprised him and ignited his own fury in response.

"You call this opportunity?" She lifted herself up to glare into his eyes.

"What are you talking about?" Daeson asked. "Rayleans can leave whenever they please...and we certainly don't murder people! You're speaking nonsense!" He glared back at her, now just inches away from her face.

The moment hung until the forgotten sound of the waves returned.

"When you risked your life to save a Colloquial, I thought you might be different," she whispered, her countenance falling. "But I guess I was wrong."

For some bizarre and unfathomable reason, Daeson was drawn to her in spite of her accusations.

"May I please be taken back now?" she asked.

Sadness enveloped him. Was this really what she thought of his people...of him?

"Of course," he responded.

She backed away and began walking to the aerobike. Once there she turned and looked at the ocean one last time. He came to stand beside her. A few moments of silence seemed to quell the tension between them.

"You're a strange girl with strange beliefs, Raviel Arko."

She took a deep breath and nodded. "Perhaps, but it is the truth that makes me so." She looked a little sad as she glanced up at him.

"Thank you for the amazing food and..." she looked out toward the water. "For a ride on the ocean."

Daeson entered Drudgetown and followed her directions. She insisted on being dropped off at the closest grav-rail terminal to her home and walking the rest of the way so as not to draw attention. As she walked away, a part of Daeson's heart went with her.

Perhaps in a different existence, he thought. But here on Jypton as Drudge and Royal, they might as well be on completely different planets.

Raviel walked slowly toward home, her heart racing. Her ploy to disable and repair Lockridge's aerobike had worked well...too well. Her encounter with him was far beyond anything the Council had advised her to do. And the words she'd spoken to him—the breach in protocol—she was done! Her actions were unforgiveable. She imagined herself trying to explain it all to the Council and cringed. Why had she done it? Something about the man propelled her forward without thinking. And why had he responded to her so? Nothing about his actions made sense, unless he truly was curious about the truth. Whatever it was, she felt as though she and her mission were in peril. She stopped and screamed at the stars in silence. She had worked so hard to get to this place, and it had all been undone in a night.

CHAPTER

5

Awakening

For the rest of the week, Daeson's class of cadets prepared for their first flight in a combat-ready A32. The armament for a fully weaponized A32 included two phaser burst guns, four concussion missiles, and two plasma cannons. Each weapon had its strengths and weaknesses. The phaser burst guns were effective against other small fighters outfitted with light- to medium-strength energy shields. The concussion missiles were used against frigate-class starships and larger. They were slow to target but packed the punch necessary to penetrate energy shields and hulls depending on their warhead. However, for most pilots, the preferred weapons of choice were the two plasma cannons positioned midway down each dual wing. Plasma cannons were slower than the phaser burst guns but faster than the concussion missiles yet still had the ability to penetrate shields and hulls as effectively as most missile warheads. And as long as the Starcraft had fuel, the self-generating plasma cannons never ran out.

Although the academics and subsequent exams were grueling, Daeson had done well. He also passed all of his simulation rides. Such was not the case for most of the rest of his class. Only eight cadets would be ready for their first flight at the beginning of the next week. Among the honored were Linden, Brehan, and Xandra. Interaction between Daeson and Xandra throughout the week was cool at best.

"What do you say we celebrate our week with a little clandestine trip to Drudgetown?" Brehan suggested with a broad smile across his chiseled face.

"Hey, this is not the time to screw up...not right before we get to fly the A32s," Daeson said.

Linden smiled. "Well, look who's playing it safe for the first time *ever*."

Daeson shook his head. "I've been waiting my whole life for this, and I don't want anything to happen that would jeopardize it."

Linden smirked. "What could happen to us in Drudgetown? I say we go. We haven't been there in a long time." He wrapped an arm around Daeson's neck. "I insist. Remember that dance club? What was the name?"

"It was the Lulu Club," Xandra answered. "And thirty seconds after you three stepped on the dance floor, everyone in the place knew you were imposters."

"Well?" Linden said, tightening his grip around Daeson's neck.

Daeson huffed and then nodded. Linden loosened his hold and looked at Xandra.

"What do you say, Xan...going to join us?" he asked.

Xandra glanced toward Daeson. The ache in her eyes was still evident, although she would never admit it. "You boys go have your fun. I'm meeting up with my cousin Sulanna tonight."

At that Brehan's eyes lit up. "Why don't you bring her with? I'll bet she's never had a drink of Drudge ale or had her life prophesied before."

Xandra's eyebrow lifted as a subtle smile crossed her lips. "Sound's fun. We'll meet you at the Orion Club."

Daeson squinted at Xandra, but she pretended not to notice.

Later when Xandra and Sulanna joined Daeson, Linden, and Brehan at the Orion Club, Xandra's scheme quickly became evident. She warmed up to Linden, much to his surprise and delight. Brehan, of course, took to Sulanna, and she didn't seem to mind at all. This left Daeson as an awkward fifth wheel. Seeing Xandra warm to Linden hurt more than he expected.

It took them over thirty minutes to lose Linden's royal guard escorts before Brehan took them to a shop near the border of Drudgetown, where, for a small fee, they were able to exchange their clothes for Drudge clothing—dark gray with minimal subdued accouterments. Dressed as Drudge, they were forced to violate the fraternization rules so they could blend in. Perhaps this was part of the thrill of visiting Drudgetown. Linden and Daeson were not often in the public eye, so the risk of their being recognized as royalty, especially while wearing Drudge clothing, was minimal.

Before long they were drinking Drudge ale at the Lulu club near the center of Drudgetown. They joined in the singing and dancing, imitating the ways of the Drudge in every way...or so they thought. Daeson mostly watched. A few girls had tried to gain his attention, but for some reason he just wasn't in the mood to talk, let alone dance. Drudge dancing was less provocative than Jyptonian. It most certainly had to do with the conservative Raylean heritage. An occasional touch of the hand was all that was allowed, yet oddly it seemed more intimate than the ways of his own people.

Daeson turned to order another ale when he caught a glimpse of a group of four that had entered the club. One girl immediately caught his eye. The way she walked was all he needed to know who it was. His heart quickened, and he scoffed at himself, dismissing any notion that this lowly mechtech could affect him thusly. He saw Raviel scan the room and recognize him. Her left eyebrow lifted above glaring eyes, but her countenance was not unpleasant. Surprise was more the emotion. Her gaze lingered, those eyes nearly ruining him.

Daeson had seen her in attire other than her mechtech uniform only once before. There was nothing remotely stylish about Drudge clothing, but Raviel made drab look good. Painted eyes, groomed dark hair hanging loosely about her shoulders—a mechtech tonight she was not. She turned to converse with the two other girls and the guy with her. After they had found a table near the far wall, Daeson watched her excuse herself and make her way to the restrooms near the back of the club.

Turning back to receive his ale from the bot server, Daeson tried to appear disinterested in Raviel's arrival. He concentrated on the unusual flavor of the ale that was growing on him each time he took another drink. The music in Drudgetown was more somber and reflective. And although the beat was not slow, there was an ache between each measure that he had never heard in any other kind of music. Epic, thirsty, haunting.

"I think you may be in the wrong club." Raviel stood next to Daeson without looking at him. She signaled the service bot for four drinks.

"Do you know what the odds are that you and I would happen to be in the same club at the same time in Drudgetown?" Daeson replied without glancing her direction.

"Makes me wonder if you aren't stalking me," Raviel responded, cutting her eyes quickly his direction to reveal an intriguing gleam. She seemed unusually relaxed which pleased Daeson. She had him at a disadvantage and knew it. His venture into Drudgetown was unexplainable to any authority, especially the royal family. She was safe here.

The shirt Raviel was wearing was cut lower on one side of her neck than the other, and Daeson caught a glimpse of a red mark on her left clavicle, except that it was more than a mark—it was an insignia of some sort.

The bot delivered the four drinks to Raviel.

"Do you need assistance serving these?" the service bot asked in its mechanical tone.

"No," Daeson said, grabbing two of the four. "I've got these."

Raviel tilted her head. "Not a good idea." Then she leaned into him. "But watching a Royal serve a table of Drudges is something I just can't pass up," she spoke quietly in his ear.

After hesitating momentarily, she grabbed the remaining two mugs of ale. Daeson followed her to the table.

"Raviel! Who's this?" one of the girls asked with a twinkle in her eye. "Where've you been hiding him?"

Raviel seemed a little flustered. She and Daeson set the ales down, and she recovered quickly. "This is

Dade. We work together at the academy. Meet my cousin, Trisk. This is Shawda and Nissy."

"Hey," Daeson said with a smile, rehearsing in his mind any nuances he'd picked up from the last couple of times he had been in Drudgetown.

"Are you a mechtech like Raviel?" Trisk asked, eyes narrow. He was large for a Drudge—stocky build, dark hair and chiseled features. He looked like he could handle himself. There was a definite resemblance to Raviel. Daeson picked up on the scrutinizing glare from Raviel.

"Yeah, but not nearly as good as she is."

Nissy scooted over on the bench seat to make room for Daeson to sit. He shrugged and sat down. She smiled and winked at Raviel, but Raviel just rolled her eyes.

"So what do you like most about your job?" Trisk asked.

"Seriously, Trisk?" Nissy glared. "You're going to grill him about his work?"

She turned back to Daeson. "What region of the city are you from. What family?"

"I'm actually new here. Got transported in from Tunadah a couple of weeks ago."

Daeson remembered hearing this from one of the mechtech foremen and hoped they would buy it.

"I know another guy from that transport," Trisk said. "Ever meet someone named Kross?"

Daeson pretended to think. "No, I don't believe I have."

"What did you say your family name was?" Trisk followed.

"Enough with the twenty questions already," Raviel said. "Dade asked me to dance earlier so..."

Daeson looked at Raviel, trying not to look shocked. "Yes...yes, let's dance."

He stood, grateful for her rescue but nervous about the dance. He wasn't very good, especially when it came to Drudge-style dancing. He followed her toward the dance floor.

"You weren't going to survive that," Raviel said.

"I know...thanks."

Raviel led him onto the floor, and she unwittingly stopped right next to Linden and Xandra—or perhaps not so unwittingly. The encounter between Xandra and Raviel when he had landed his Starcraft after saving Tig a week earlier quickly flashed through his mind. Was Raviel goading Xandra? Xandra scowled at Raviel and then at Daeson, but his partner seemed unaware. Linden raised an eyebrow after watching the exchange.

Raviel leaned close to Daeson. "Watch me closely," she whispered.

She lifted the back of her hand to Daeson, and he followed. The backs of their hands touched, and Daeson shivered. Perhaps it was the taboo of touching a Drudge, but something told him it was more than that. They moved in sync with the music in an elegant rhythm of steps and spins. Daeson quickly learned and captured the movement of the dance, anticipating each time the backs of their hands were allowed to touch.

The disdainful looks from Xandra drifted away, along with everyone else near them. In their own world of intimacy, he and Raviel moved in perfect synchronicity. With each twist and turn, the distance between them diminished, and their eyes never left each other. Her gaze seemed to freeze and heighten his senses in a way he had never experienced. As the music swelled toward its finale, the last touch arrived, and Raviel turned the palm of her hand to Daeson. Their eyes locked as he turned his hand to hers. Palm to palm they finished the dance, and Daeson was taken. The final note faded away, but he did not drop his hand, and neither did she. Who was this lowly girl that undid him so? Slowly their hands fell, but he prolonged the touch until their fingers briefly but intimately interlocked before parting.

Daeson could hardly move, his eyes fixed on hers. He felt her breath on his cheek. A brief but intense silent moment entwined them.

"I need to get back to my friends," Raviel whispered.

"Yes," Daeson replied. It was all he could say.

Raviel turned and walked away just as a quiet voice laced with scorn fell on his ears.

"She is why you refuse me? A lowly Drudge?" Xandra's eyes burned with fury.

Daeson turned to see that Linden had left and was moving toward the bar to order ale. Daeson tried to respond to Xandra, but words would only condemn him further. She snapped her back toward him and followed Linden. Daeson made his way to a table and waited for the evening to expire, his thoughts continually turning to the dance with Raviel and his emotions in a mess of confusion.

Brehan and Linden sensed the new tension in the group. Daeson tried to leave, but they would have none of it. Instead, they convinced everyone to have their lives prophesied by a Drudge oracle to lighten the mood. After a mild protest, Daeson and the two girls yielded. They found an oracle not far from the club, and each in turn went in to the prophecy lounge and exited with wild stories about their futures that brought great amusement to them all.

Daeson tried to refuse once more, but the group wouldn't allow it. He entered the oracle's lounge, expecting to see bizarre displays of mystical elements, oils, incense, and a gypsy-esque fortune teller. And that is exactly what he saw. He sat down across from the old woman and could hardly keep from laughing. But before she could speak, a young woman with white hair and wise eyes entered. Her dark gray cloak covered mundane clothing, not at all like the other woman's attire. The original oracle stood and exited without saying a word. The white-haired oracle stood in silence for a moment before sitting down and looking deep into the Daeson's eyes. Any levity in his heart vanished, and he could hardly bear her gaze.

"Your Elite friends think this..." she motioned to the room about them, "...amusing and absurd. And so it is...but I am not. My name is Sabella, and I am here only because you are here." Her voice was slow and deliberate.

Daeson tried to laugh but couldn't. He tried to look away but couldn't. He tried to stand up and leave but couldn't.

"What I am about to speak to you is truth. I am no mystic, neither do I claim to be clairvoyant. I am simply a messenger."

At that, Sabella's eyes narrowed. "Royal blood flows through your veins, but you are not who you think you are. Soon there is coming a day when the facade of your life will be discovered. You are set apart to turn sorrow into joy for many people and joy into sorrow for many more."

The words landed on Daeson's ears with numbness, as if he were listening to someone read poetry to an audience. Realism denied him an immediate response, but the absolute sincerity and soberness with which the oracle spoke commanded his attention.

"Your struggle will be long and painful, but do not be afraid. Sovereign Ell Yon will guide you and protect you."

Daeson forced a smile onto his lips and pointed a finger at the woman. "Your riddles are just foolish babblings. But then again, that's why we came here, isn't it?"

Sabella didn't react. As Daeson's right hand came to rest on the table, the oracle grabbed his wrist with her left hand. Before he could react, she pressed a miniature genetic scanner into his palm, which extracted a few subdermal cells. He pulled his hand back, appalled that this crazy Drudge woman had touched him. The oracle read the scanner and then pressed a button on the device before closing it and stowing it away in an inside pocket on her cloak.

"Your genetics are poisoned by Deitum Prime, but it isn't enough to mask your origins. Daeson Lockridge, are you afraid to know the truth?"

Daeson's eyes lifted as chills covered his body. "How do you know my name?"

Sabella tilted her head slightly. "I know much more about you than your name. Are you afraid...afraid of the truth?"

Whatever ruse the woman was playing was working on him. He wanted to leave but could not overcome the desire to hear more. His conversation with Raviel days earlier about being deceived came back to him.

"I'm not afraid." But he was.

Without a signal, the oracle's apprentice came through the sliding door and handed her a glass tablet. She turned it toward Daeson. "This is your genetic scan.

The Jyptonian database identifying you as Daeson Lockridge has been altered." She swiped the database away, and it was replaced with a different one.

"This is our untainted Raylean database. You can see that you are..." Sabella hesitated and looked straight into Daeson's soul. "One hundred percent Raylean. Your family name is Starlore of the Jahrim Clan."

Daeson slowly nodded. "I see. Did Linden or Brehan set this up? They should have tried something a little more believable. You had me going for a while."

Daeson stood up and began laughing, but the woman just stared back at him.

"Okay, thank you for the amusement. It was well worth it." He spun about and left the lounge. As he went to join his friends outside, he broadened his smile and began laughing heartily. He decided to twist their ruse back on them by telling a completely different and wildly absurd fortune that he made up on the spot. But much to his surprise, none of them seemed disappointed or called him on the made-up story that didn't match the oracle's. Daeson wasn't quite sure what to make of what had just happened.

The group made a stop at another Drudge club, but Daeson found no pleasure in it. The oracle had stolen his joy away. He left early and found his way back to his aerobike. The words of the white-haired woman continued to eat away at him as the lights of Athlone streaked by, the whine of the aerobike steadily rising in pitch along with his speed. On the outskirts of the city, Daeson opened up the throttle. The two full moons gave ample light to navigate without activating the night vision on his helmet. The landscape became a blur as he fled the lies behind him, but he couldn't outrun the truth before him. The oracle's words echoed through his mind until nothing else occupied the halls of his thought.

When he finally found his way home at the late night hour, he quietly entered his mother's bedchamber. Her chest slowly rose and fell with each breath. Something was already different. He stood silent for a long time, remembering that as a boy all he had to do to wake her was to stand beside her slumbering form and look at her. Within minutes she would open her eyes and ask what was the matter. Wasn't that proof enough of a mother's biological connection to her son?

Daeson knelt down beside her bed so that he could clearly see her beautiful face...so peaceful...so loving.

"Mother," he whispered.

Saskia instantly opened her eyes to see Daeson before her.

"Who am I?"

CHAPTER

5

Origins

I have seen the burden of your captivity and heard the cries of your children. I will not forget my covenant with Rayl and will set you free from the bondage of Jypton. – Micaba, Oracle of Ell Yon.

"They couldn't fix me." Daeson's mother cradled the chalice of warm viscalli tea that he had made for her. "I desperately wanted a child to call my own."

Daeson sat down next to her on her bed. She looked up and touched his cheek.

For Jyptonian women who wanted children, the fertilized embryo was immediately transplanted to a perfectly controlled simulated uterus. Here the child was nourished with a perfect supply of nutrients and of course Deitum Prime until the day of birth. At that time the mother and her family would receive the child into their home. For the wealthy, this arrival might be delayed a number of years so as not to inconvenience the family. The process was a significant improvement since the woman was not subjected to the pain or inconvenience of natural childbirth. But for a select few women who could not become pregnant, these birthing centers could do little to help. And as advanced as Jypton's medical knowledge was, there were still some medical conditions that eluded them.

"What happened, mother?" Daeson said, reaching for her hand. "I need to know."

Saskia took a deep breath and looked away into the echoes of her past. Her face revealed such sadness when she turned back to Daeson.

"Are you sure?"

Daeson thought about that question. Clearly there was a truth that could change everything. Did he really want to know it? He nodded.

Saskia straightened her back and lowered her head. She looked so regal...so perfectly royal. Yet there was a tenderness about her that eluded all of the rest of the palace.

"I knew this day would come. I was hoping it would be much later. Years ago your father and I were walking in the Gardens of Athlone. He was trying to lift my spirits—it was the only place that seemed to help. The palace only made me feel worse." Saskia offered a weak smile. "Alleanna would soon receive Linden from the birthing center, and as the day drew close, I became despondent, knowing that forever I would be childless. Experiencing such jealousy towards the Chancellor and Alleanna made me feel all the worse. As your father and I sat on one of the benches near the edge of the garden, a young Drudge woman burst through the hedges behind us. She was terrified."

Saskia paused as her eyes grew distant. Daeson imagined that his mother was remembering the vivid details of the moment...details that could never fully be described—the wide eyes of the woman, the smells of the garden, the color of tears, and the sound of fear.

"She came directly to me, even though your father tried to stop her. When he saw what she was carrying, he loosened his grip, and the woman fell to her knees before me, eyes wide with fear. 'Please...please take my son,' she pleaded. Her eyes filled with tears when she looked into the sweet little face of her baby.

"'Why? What's wrong?' I asked. She was frantically looking all around her and back to her child. 'He's been marked for termination! Please take him, save him!' and then she put the baby in my arms."

Dark thoughts began to form in Daeson's mind that made him shudder. "Termination?" he asked slowly.

Daeson's mother looked at him with eyes that wore the burden of dark knowledge. "As you know, every one born on Jypton is registered in the population database. The Drudge often have babies with genome defects. It's believed that their weak genetics make them only capable of performing servant caste duties. When a Drudge child is born, it is tested for these defects by our genetics and registration drones."

The realization of what his mother was saying horrified him. Pieces of his conversations with Raviel came back to him, along with the anger she had expressed toward him that had caught him by surprise. Perhaps Raviel wasn't lying after all. He shook his head and turned away.

"It's believed that too great a number of genetically defective Drudge would cripple our society. The Chancellor believes it is far better and merciful to reduce these social burdens early. It's a solution that has been used for hundreds of years."

As the reality of the words she had spoken sunk in, Daeson became angry. He turned back to his mother, eyes fierce with repulsion. "And you believe this, mother?"

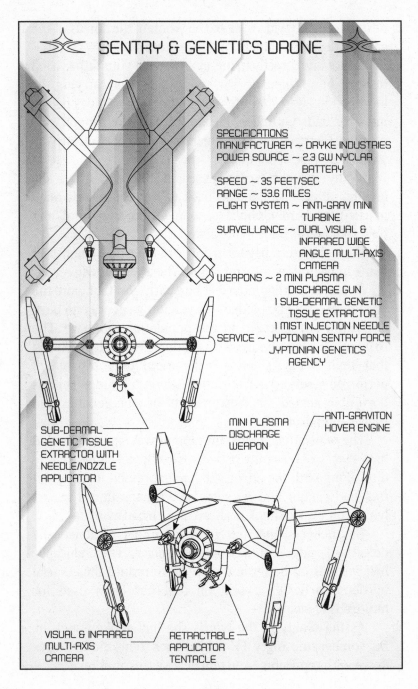

SENTRY & GENETICS DRONE

SPECIFICATIONS
MANUFACTURER ~ DRYKE INDUSTRIES
POWER SOURCE ~ 2.3 GW NYCLAR
BATTERY
SPEED ~ 35 FEET/SEC
RANGE ~ 53.6 MILES
FLIGHT SYSTEM ~ ANTI-GRAV MINI
TURBINE
SURVEILLANCE ~ DUAL VISUAL &
INFRARED WIDE
ANGLE MULTI-AXIS
CAMERA
WEAPONS ~ 2 MINI PLASMA
DISCHARGE GUN
1 SUB-DERMAL GENETIC
TISSUE EXTRACTOR
1 MIST INJECTION NEEDLE
SERVICE ~ JYPTONIAN SENTRY FORCE
JYPTONIAN GENETICS
AGENCY

SUB-DERMAL
GENETIC TISSUE
EXTRACTOR WITH
NEEDLE/NOZZLE
APPLICATOR

MINI PLASMA
DISCHARGE
WEAPON

ANTI-GRAVITON
HOVER ENGINE

VISUAL & INFRARED
MULTI-AXIS
CAMERA

RETRACTABLE
APPLICATOR
TENTACLE

Saskia turned away from Daeson's hard stare. "I did," she whispered. "Until that night...the night *you* came into my life."

She turned back and looked into Daeson's eyes. Hers were moist. "While I was holding you, genetics drones came." Saskia shook her head. "But they do more than sample genetics. When the woman ran, they pursued. She only made it a few feet before one attached to her back and injected her with a substance called the Mist. She died within seconds, and then they came for you."

Tears began to spill onto Saskia's cheeks. "Your father drew his Talon and took out two of them, but a third nearly made it to you. In that moment when I saw your beautiful, perfect little face, I became a mother. Something welled up so strong inside me that I don't even now understand it. I covered you with my body, waiting for the Mist to inject or spray, but it didn't happen. When I dared look up, I saw your father kneeling on the ground. Beneath his hand was a smashed drone."

Saskia bit her lip as tears flowed down her beautiful face. She made no attempt to wipe them away. "His bleeding hand had absorbed some of the Mist, and he fell ill." She shook her head. "Though he was with us for ten more years, he never fully recovered."

Daeson's eyes widened. "Is that why he—" he could hardly say the word, "died when I was just a boy?"

Saskia said nothing. She just reached for Daeson's hand, and he folded her hand in his, wrapping an arm around her as she leaned into him. He held her for a long time, comforting the broken heart of his mother.

"I'm not Jyptonian. I'm a genetically defective... Drudge." Daeson's voice felt hoarse and foreign...not his own. Was anything his own now?

Saskia sat up straight and wiped away her tears.

"No! Not defective. We took you away to a distant city, where your father was able to place you in a birthing center for the appropriate time of delivery. When I told the palace that I had become pregnant and had delayed telling anyone because we didn't want to detract from the birth and delivery of the royal prince, we received you one year later without question. You were tested, and your genetics were perfect. Your father was able to have the Jyptonian database adjusted so as not to flag your actual heritage. You had become our very own child, and we loved you as such."

"But I'm not!" Daeson stated firmly, standing up and walking away. "I'm nothing more than a mere Drudge!"

Saskia came to him and shushed him. She held on to him tightly and looked him directly in the eyes. "You are my son, and nothing in the galaxy will ever change that. You will continue to be my son. No one ever need know, Daeson. You are of the royal family of Jypton...do you understand!"

It was more than a plea. Daeson wanted to run...run from the lies. He looked down at the face of Saskia and realized that even though his world had just been turned upside down, she did indeed love him as a son. He hugged his mother, but something was different now.

CHAPTER

7

Forced Fate

Quantum Entanglement – a phenomenon in which two or more particles remain entangled or connected so that actions performed on one instantly affect the other, even when separated by great distances.

T wo days later, after the cadets returned from break, Daeson waited until the activity in the Starcraft hangar was minimal before walking toward Raviel's T32 as if he were on a mission. When he reached the Starcraft, he found her up on a step ladder platform, leaning into the cockpit.

"Hey...I need to talk to you."

Raviel straightened. She was holding a flight processor interface module that was tethered via a cable to the data port in the cockpit. Raviel wiped her brow with the back of her hand. Her eyes narrowed and then she stiffened.

"Yes, sir. The repairs for this Starcraft are nearly complete. We expect to have it back on the flight schedule by the middle of next week."

Daeson's brow furrowed.

"Can I help you, sir?" Daeson spun about to see a Colloquial mechtech foreman approaching. The foreman's eyes widened when he saw that he was addressing not just another academy cadet but a member of the royal family.

Daeson smiled. "No. I'm just checking on the status of the Starcraft I nearly ruined."

"Not so, sir." The foreman shook his head. "From what I heard, you saved that cadet's life."

Since the event, Daeson had earned the respect of every Colloquial at the academy, evidently including the maintenance staff.

"We can easily deal with a few repairs on a Starcraft if it brings our pilots back safely."

"I appreciate that, Foreman..." Daeson leaned forward to read his nametag. "...Harel. Would you mind if I ask your mechtech a few questions regarding the repairs? I'd like to learn what happens when a Starcraft is pushed to its limits like that. I think it will make me a better pilot."

"Absolutely, Master Lockridge. Take as much time as you need. She's one of our best, so I'm sure she'll be able to help you."

"You don't say." Daeson raised a skeptical eyebrow and shot a quick glance up toward Raviel. "Thank you, Harel."

The foreman saluted and walked on. Raviel smirked and shook her head as Daeson climbed the step ladder to join her on the platform.

"What are you doing?" she asked in hushed tones as Daeson came close to her. "What do you want from me? Don't you realize what this will do to me?" She glanced up at him. She tried to look angry but her eyes belied her. "Please just leave me alone."

Daeson couldn't help seeing her as his beautiful dance partner. He nodded to the cockpit and leaned over the rail. Raviel reluctantly joined him. They were side by side now, just inches apart. She pointed and held up the interface module as if explaining something to him. The distinctive smell of lubricants, fuel, and plasma residue on Raviel did nothing to diminish the flutter of responses he was having. That final moment of the Drudge dance had changed him.

"I need to talk to you." He looked deep into her eyes.

Raviel seemed a little stunned. "I'd say you've orchestrated enough of a ruse to do just that. What do you want...really?"

"Not here...not now. I want to meet you off campus."

At that, Raviel pulled back with widened eyes. Her body tensed, and her eyes narrowed at him once more. "Master Lockridge, you have the power to destroy my life. Please just leave me alone. You risk too much by talking to me like this."

Daeson continued to stare at her before looking back to the innards of the cockpit. Perhaps she was right. He was tempted to stuff the truth away and move on, but...

"And what of the other night...the dance?"

Raviel hung her head. "That never happened. Please go," Raviel said without looking up.

Daeson slowly nodded and tried to leave but couldn't. Not now, knowing who he was...what he was. She was his only link to a world he knew nothing of.

"You said I was deceived, that not everything was as it seems." He hesitated. "That I was different than most Elite."

Raviel looked over at him.

"I think you may be right, and I need to talk to you. Will you meet me?"

Raviel searched his eyes.

"Please," he added.

She took a deep breath and then looked right and left.

"Do you know where the Mod Exchange in Drudgetown is?"

"East of the transit grav-rail?" Daeson asked.

"That's it. Go to Kyson's Bot-Mod—the third hour."

Daeson nodded. "I know I'm asking a lot of you. Thank you."

Daeson and Raviel did a quick walk around the Starcraft to finish up the mock inspection before he left.

Raviel jumped back up to the cockpit platform with her flight processor interface module and plugged it into the port, intentionally not looking at Lockridge as he walked away from her Starcraft. She found it impossible to concentrate, so she mindlessly paged through menus and data fields while trying to process what had just happened. That dance with him had done its job well. This is exactly what the Council of the Plexus had been hoping for. Unfortunately, the effects were double-edged. She had not been trained for this...this emotional seduction they were asking of her. She found herself becoming angry for softening toward Lockridge. She had to constantly remind herself of what he represented, what he believed, and the millions of Rayleans who had died at the hands of his family.

"Steel your heart, Raviel!" she said under her breath. "And get back to work."

It worked for a few minutes, but back in the corner of her mind, she couldn't help but wonder—no, hope—that Lockridge was indeed different. That was something she would never reveal to the Plexus. It would mean the end of her mission as a spy for her people. Meeting Lockridge privately off campus was extremely dangerous. For a moment she considered the possibility that he was actually playing her, that perhaps he was suspicious of her activity and interest, and that she was walking into a trap. She would have to communicate this to the Plexus via her quantum entanglement communicator or QEC. The Plexus would make the call as to whether the risk was worth it.

Time was of the essence. She found an excuse to go to her locker and quickly sent the secret message. She would finish her shift before checking for a response. Hoping the reply would be negative, she feared the outcome of such a meeting, no matter what the response was.

Late that night, Daeson made his way back to Drudgetown and donned the dull clothing once more, sinking a little deeper underneath his hood. On his previous visits to Drudgetown, he was pretty sure that he and his friends hadn't fooled anyone, but they had their fun and left. This was different. For a Royal to be in Drudgetown alone would raise suspicion that would be very difficult to explain if reported. This time, his entrance into Drudgetown felt different. He noticed things he'd never seen before. Things he hadn't given a second thought to before now wore on him.

He bought a drink at the shop across the street from Kyson's Bot-Mod and sat at an outdoor table so he could watch. In spite of the dark and early hour, the street was quite busy. A subculture of night people created a completely different impression in any city sector, whether Drudge or Elite.

Daeson watched a young man escort a pregnant woman, presumably his wife, down the walkway. He didn't often see pregnant women, only in Drudgetown. When he did, he was always intrigued and mystified by the Rayleans' insistence on childbearing naturally. The distortion to the female body, as well as the loss of mobility, function, and freedom, astounded him. *Why would they subject themselves to such a thing so unnecessarily?* He wondered and then imagined his real mother carrying him inside her, bearing the pain of natural childbirth, only to lose him hours later. His chest squeezed. He shook himself away from the thoughts that had plagued him for the last few days since his conversations with the oracle and then his mother.

Daeson took a sip of his drink as a sentry slowly glided down the street on a patrol aerobike. Nearly every conversation between Drudges stopped as he passed. A surveillance drone hovered near his shoulder. Sentries carried two small drones, one in each of the docking stations on the forearms of their armored uniforms. It was an efficient method of expanding each sentry's area of responsibility. Surveillance cameras in Drudgetown always seemed to malfunction within days after their installation; hovering drones were their answer to the rebellious annoyance of such sabotage. Besides this, surveillance cameras had blind spots—hovering drones had none. Colloquial sentries were hated among the Drudge, and Daeson now suspected that it had to do with not only the abuse Raviel spoke of, but also the fact that the sentries were a constant reminder of the Rayleans' subjugation to the Jyptonians.

Daeson saw Raviel approach Kyson's Bot-Mod. She stopped and looked in all directions until she spotted Daeson across the street. She tapped something on a glass tablet and then scanned up and down the street multiple times before approaching him. She looked nervous. Daeson stood and pulled out a chair for Raviel. The only other person he had ever done that for was his mother; it felt awkward and right at the same time. Raviel's face was difficult to read, and she hesitated before allowing him to seat her. Daeson returned to his seat across the table.

"Would you like something to drink?" he asked.

Raviel shook her head. She looked blankly at him, and for a moment he just stared back at her. What he was about to tell her would change the course of his life forever. After this conversation, there was no going back. His secret would be out and impossible to silence. Could he trust her? He knew so little about her and yet...

Daeson opened his mouth, but Raviel was first to speak.

"Before you say anything, I need to know...why me?" Her eyes narrowed...waiting.

"Because other than my estate servant, you are my only link to the Dru...Rayleans that I can trust."

Raviel squinted. "You don't know me at all. How can you possibly say you trust me?"

"When we danced...I knew. And because I've already put my life in your hands many times. If the academy trusts you to work on my Starcraft, then I can trust you too."

Raviel glared at him, stone-faced. She seemed so cold compared to a few nights ago at the club.

"It's *my* Starcraft," she said without batting an eye.

Daeson tilted his head toward her in acknowledgment.

He took a deep breath. "Look...I know this isn't fair to you, and I don't expect anything from you...I just need to tell someone. I need someone to help me process this—"

Raviel shook her head as two dark figures walked by.

"Not here," she said once the men were clear.

She stood up. "Follow me."

Raviel turned and walked up the street. Daeson stepped in pace beside her. They walked for quite a distance, turning left and right multiple times until they ended in an alley behind a row of common dwellings. The streets here were empty, amidst a slumbering community and away from the nightlife of the Mod-Exchange. Raviel pulled out her glass tablet from her cloak, tapping a few times before returning it.

She looked directly at Daeson. "This should be safe."

Daeson nodded. "Not sure where to start." He took another deep breath and seriously considered walking away. He could pretend for the rest of his life, couldn't he?

Raviel waited patiently. She looked tired. Daeson looked across the alley toward a light in a window.

"That night after we danced, my friends insisted that we go to see one of your oracles...just as a gag. Each of us went in and came out laughing."

Daeson lowered his head and then looked up at Raviel. "But inside, I wasn't laughing. What she said really rattled me."

"What did she tell you?" Raviel asked.

"She immediately knew I was of the royal family, but she said I was not who I thought I was. She told me that one day soon the facade of my life would be discovered but not to be afraid for I was destined to turn sorrow into joy for many people. And then she said that my struggle would be long and painful, but Sovereign Ell Yon would guide me."

Daeson paused long enough for Raviel to respond, but she stayed silent...pondering.

He huffed. "I don't even know who Sovereign Ell Yon is! I told the oracle that her words were foolish and nonsense, and to me they were. But then she grabbed my hand and swiped a genetic scanner across my palm before I could pull it away."

Daeson lifted his hand and looked at it, remembering not the scan so much as the oracle's touch. "I guess she knew I would never report her."

Continuing his story, Daeson began with the oracle's words: "'Your genetics are poisoned by Deitum Prime, but it isn't enough to mask your origins.'" Then he added, "Her eyes fairly pierced my soul." When Daeson closed his eyes, he could still see the woman's hazel eyes probing him.

"She asked if I was afraid to know the truth. I said no and then she showed me a Raylean database depicting my heritage as one hundred percent..." He hesitated, "Raylean!"

Daeson looked back at Raviel. Her eyes widened.

"I still didn't believe what she had said, but it shook me up so much that when I joined my friends, I made up some absurd fortune that we all laughed at." He rubbed his brow with his hand. Sharing the story had unsettled him.

"Some claiming to be oracles are frauds, but my people don't deal lightly with them. What was the name of the oracle you saw?" Raviel asked.

Daeson thought for a moment. "Sa...Sabel I think."

"Sabella?" Raviel asked.

"Yes...that's it...Sabella. Why?"

Raviel's face became sober. "Whatever she told you..." She looked deep into Daeson's eyes and added, "...is true. She's never been wrong...never!"

Daeson turned and leaned against the wall where they were standing, relying on the wall to hold him up. "I believe you because that night I confronted my mother." He turned his head and looked at Raviel again. She slowly lifted her hand to her mouth. Out of nowhere, tears welled up in Daeson's eyes but did not spill. After retelling Raviel the story of his rescue as an infant, he fell silent. Eventually he looked over at her.

"She wants me to just keep living this lie." Daeson shook his head. "I...I don't know what to do."

"If you're not the son of a Royal Lockridge, then to which family do you belong?"

Somehow, speaking his story to Raviel made it so much more real.

"My name is Starlore. I'm no Royal prince...I'm just a Drudge!"

Raviel turned and stepped in front of him so they were face to face. He hung his head, covering his face with his hands. She gently put her hands on his wrists and pulled them down. Her smile soothed his pain. Even in the dim of the night in a murky alley, her eyes shone bright with compassion.

"If this is true, then you're not a Drudge...you're Raylean. And one day you'll understand the courageous legacy and hopeful future that encompasses."

Daeson drew strength from this lowly Raylean girl. He tilted his head back and looked up to the stars, and that's when he saw it.

"Raviel!" he whispered. "A surveillance drone!"

She looked up. The silent sentry was hovering ten feet above them. As soon as it captured the image of her face, it bolted down the alley. Raviel pulled the glass tablet from her cloak. Her fingers flew across it, tapping in rapid sequences.

"I'm through!" Daeson said. "This will cause a global scandal. My mother...they'll imprison her or worse! It's over!"

"Not yet, it's not," Raviel said defiantly. "Come on!" She bolted down the alley after the drone, holding her tablet before her.

Daeson took out after her.

"What's the point? Wherever this thing is going, it's already transmitted our entire conversation. I'm sure the captain of the surveillance force is already watching it."

Raviel ran faster, and Daeson had to work to keep up with her.

"I've been transmitting a jamming signal tuned to the surveillance drone's frequency, but we've got to stay close enough to keep it working." Just then the drone stopped and flew in a wide circle before them.

"What's it doing?" Daeson asked.

"I'm disrupting its navigation signal too...it's searching for its sentry, and he won't be far away," Raviel acknowledged. "We have to take it out before it finds him and downloads the recording."

They were nearly beneath the drone when it bolted again.

"Do you have your Talon with you?" Raviel asked as she continued to monitor and interact with her tablet.

"Of course," Daeson replied. He donned leather gloves and drew the Talon from its sheath. He pressed the button to charge the energy weapon.

"If you get close enough, use the blade. Don't fire unless you absolutely have to. It will draw attention," Raviel said between breaths.

Daeson extended the blade to full length as they sprinted after the drone. It was only about the size of his hand, so he would have to be precise. The drone stopped again.

"Get ready!" Raviel said. "I'm going to simulate a sentry homing signal and draw it in." She ducked behind a corner of a building and pulled Daeson in beside her. She tapped on the tablet, and they waited. The seconds ticked by. Raviel watched the graphics on her tablet and held up three fingers, two fingers, one finger—Daeson poised.

The surveillance drone glided out from around the corner, just three feet above them, and Daeson struck. The stasis sword edge of the Talon struck the drone in a splay of blue and orange sparks. It careened back and down. Daeson pursued as it impacted the ground, but it bounced back up. He sliced again, but the unstable flight path was difficult to predict, and he missed. He heard a faint but familiar electronic charging sound and recovered from his over-extended cut to make another slice. Just then the drone recovered and turned to face him five feet away at eye level. At the same instant, he realized that the drone was discharging a plasma round—Raviel dove at him from the side. The impact moved them both out of the way of the plasma burst at the last split second, and they tumbled to the ground. Daeson instinctively moved his Talon down and away from their fall while grabbing on to Raviel to protect her from the impact of the ground. His body took the brunt of the fall as she lay on top of him.

"This thing has weapons?" He asked, his face just inches from hers.

"Guess so," she answered and then rolled off him and onto her feet in an instant.

"That would have been nice to know!" he interjected as he regained his feet and ran beside her after the fleeing drone. Its flight was erratic now.

"It's the new model," she explained, tracking the drone on her tablet again. "It wouldn't have killed you. Its power module is too small, but it would have left a nasty scar."

"How do you know all of this?" Daeson asked.

"We may be the servants of Jypton, but we're not stupid. We designed much of the tech used all over this planet." Raviel tapped a few more times on the tablet. "It's adapting...we have to hurry!"

They sprinted down another alley, pursuing the drone at a frenzied pace. Daeson retracted his Talon's blade and charged the plasma chamber. They were slowly gaining on the injured drone, but it was still ten paces ahead. It exited the alley just ahead of them and turned right. Daeson and Raviel sprinted around the corner and came face to face with the sentry that had deployed the drone. It was docking on his forearm as a second drone was launching from his other forearm. The sentry was as shocked as they were, and he reached for his Talon.

Daeson didn't hesitate. All he could think about was stopping the drone from uploading its incriminating data. He charged the sentry while tossing his Talon to Raviel. The impact sent the two men tumbling to the ground, and in the ruckus Daeson ripped the docking drone from the sentry's forearm and smashed it against the ground. He heard his Talon discharge a couple of times in the distance, hoping it was Raviel taking out the second drone, but did she even know how to use a Talon?

The sentry smashed a heavy gloved fist into Daeson's head, which sent his world spinning. Daeson drove an open palm into the sentry's helmet, but it did little to impede the sentry's fighting ability. Grabbing the wrist of the sentry to prevent another blow, he then heard the sentry's Talon charging. The sentry had drawn the Talon and was bringing it to bear on Daeson's chest. Only now did Daeson realize he was in a fight not only for his reputation but also for his very life.

In the split second that remained, Daeson pushed the Talon forcefully, deflecting it away from his chest as it discharged. The plasma burst obliterated a corner of a nearby building, sending fragments of concrete everywhere. Soon there would be witnesses. The men were still locked in each other's grip, flailing across the concrete walkway when the sentry ended up on top of Daeson. Another blast would be coming soon, so Daeson let loose of the sentry's wrist to add a second hand to the Talon. The sentry did the same, and an intense struggle for control of the weapon ensued.

Daeson looked for Raviel, but she was nowhere to be found. He heard another Talon discharge in the distance. The sentry's finger covered the firing trigger, its chamber charged and ready. He had the advantage. Daeson slid his hand down just far enough to reach the blade extension trigger. A powerful twist and one split second later, the blue-tipped blade extended up and through the armor of the sentry, his eyes bulging.

Daeson felt the man's strength completely dissipate—
he fell lifeless onto Daeson's chest.

"Daeson...Daeson!" Raviel's voice echoed through
his mind as he tried to process what had just happened.
He pushed the sentry off of him and recovered to one
knee. He was breathing hard and his body felt so very
heavy. Raviel was tugging on his arm.

"Come on, Daeson...we have to get out of here!"

But then she paused and looked closer at the
sentry. She let loose of Daeson and knelt down beside
the lifeless body, grabbing his arm and tapping quickly
across the flexible glass display attached to his
forearm. Lights began illuminating the windows of the
surrounding buildings.

"We have to move now!" she urged and then
coerced him to follow her back down the alley. They
passed by the second drone, its innards splayed on the
ground, sparks occasionally arcing from its power
module. They ran. They ran until Daeson's chest hurt.
Each step carried him further from his crime and
further from the perfect life he thought he once had.
When they stopped, they were far from where he had
killed the sentry. Distant sirens filled the air, but so far
there had been no pursuit that he could identify. Raviel
pulled him into an alcove, and they both labored to
catch their breath. Daeson bent over with his hands on
his knees.

"What have I done?" he asked, shaking his head. He
stood up and began pacing.

Raviel said nothing. What could she say? She was
an accomplice to the murder of a sentry in
Drudgetown. He stopped and looked at her, observing
her fear.

"I'm sorry...I'm sorry...it just got out of hand so
quickly!"

Daeson stopped pacing, leaned up against the wall of the alcove, and slowly slid down to sit on his haunches, his hands covering his face. "I can't believe I just killed a sentry!"

His world was collapsing around him, and he felt buried in the rubble. He fought against the panic that was threatening to swallow him. His hands were shaking, and he could not process one coherent thought.

Raviel slid down the wall to sit beside him on his right. For some reason, it helped. At the very least, her action said, *I'm not abandoning you*. Daeson's mind ran wild with worst-case speculation about what would happen—he and his mother's imprisonment or even execution, the global scandal that would engulf the royal family. How far would this go? He turned and looked at Raviel. She was staring off into the distance at nothing. His worry and sadness deepened when he thought of her.

"Look what I've done to you."

She turned and looked into his eyes. "We have quite a mess, don't we?"

"I'm so sorry, Raviel. In all my life I never imagined....I have destroyed not only my life but yours as well."

Raviel remained silent.

Daeson hung his head. She reached over and gently put a hand on his arm. The rim of the rising sun could be seen between the shimmering towers of Athlone's cityscape. The day was beginning, the dawn of a new reality for Daeson. Rays of sunlight pushed against their skin, urging them into a day most difficult. Both remained silent for a while longer, contemplating their next action.

"We have no choice," Raviel finally said. "We have to keep on as if everything is normal."

Daeson looked over at her. "Normal? Seriously?"

Raviel nodded. She seemed so sure. She stood up and reached a hand down for Daeson to grab.

"Even if that were possible, which it's not, there had to have been half a dozen witnesses after those Talon discharges," Daeson argued.

"Do you think for a moment that the Colloquial sentry forces are going to find one single Drudge witness that is going to help them find another Drudge that killed a sentry? And besides that, what witness would recognize a member of the royal family fighting with a sentry at night in Drudgetown?"

Daeson thought about that. "Perhaps you're right."

Raviel nodded.

As Daeson replayed the horror of the engagement with the sentry, he remembered something.

"Hey, how do you know how to use a Talon?"

Raviel shrugged. "Point and shoot, right?"

Daeson huffed. "In theory, but it takes quite a bit of practice to hit something, especially a flying drone!"

"I guess it was a lucky shot," she replied.

Daeson nodded. "I've got to get to my aerobike soon, or it's going to look suspicious. What's the fastest way there?" he asked.

"Probably the transit grav-rail...there's a station not far from here," Raviel pointed. "Thankfully it's in the opposite direction."

Daeson took another deep breath, trying to rally the courage to move forward. He turned and faced Raviel. Were it not for her quick thinking and incredible tech skill, his life would already be over. He reached up and touched her cheek. She was difficult to read, but she didn't retreat from him. The forbidden touch was something they both seemed to need.

"No matter what happens, I'll do everything in my power to protect you," Daeson promised.

The corner of Raviel's mouth turned up ever so slightly. She glanced toward the rising sun. "You'd better go."

Daeson nodded, turned, and ran.

CHAPTER

8

The Facade

Omegeon — an element created by the Omega Nebula that emits a subatomic particle with energy levels exceeding all other known particles. Without extreme shielding, minimal exposure to Omegeon particles is deadly to all life. Miniature Omegeon crystals are extremely rare and contain massive quantities of Omegeon particles. Application uses of Omegeon are largely unknown.

Daeson's first flight in the A32 was a near disaster, his dream shattered by a destroyed future. He could hardly fly the Starcraft, let alone deploy any weapons. The debrief was two hours of humiliation and retribution. The instructor was furious and did little to hide his anger. Linden was his flight mate, and Daeson could tell he was quietly gloating.

"You were dangerous out there, cadet Lockridge. I expected much more than that. You fly like that again tomorrow, and you'll be done!"

After the instructor left the briefing room, Linden eyed Daeson.

"What's going on, Daeson?" Linden asked. "Something's eating you...you know you can tell me anything."

Daeson shook his head. "I'm okay."

Linden continued to stare. "You haven't started something foolish with that Drudge we saw you dance with a few nights ago, have you?"

Daeson snapped his head toward Linden. "Are you kidding? You know me better than that!"

Linden smirked. "Well, Xandra's sure done with you." He stood up. "Your loss is my gain, I guess." He slapped Daeson on the shoulder and exited the room.

Linden's words felt like a knife cutting deep into his soul. It was the first time ever that Linden had mentioned Xandra's affection for him. Daeson sighed and dropped his head. He had no friends. Somewhere along the way, Linden's relationship had become a pretense, along with everything else in his life.

The next few days gave Daeson no relief from his misery. Every second of every day he fully expected the sentries or the Royal Guard or both to burst into his classroom or home and arrest him for murder, not to mention his impersonating a member of the royal family. The guilt, fear, and apprehension were nearly unbearable. He convinced himself that what he'd done was in self-defense, but would the authorities see it that way? Would the Chancellor? Linden? And Daeson didn't dare contact Raviel for fear of discovery. Drudgetown was being torn apart as the investigation by the sentries commenced. They would be ruthless in their attempts to find the perpetrator.

As the days became weeks, Daeson's apprehension assuaged a bit, but his feelings of guilt remained. To keep from losing his mind, he tried to immerse himself in the tactical training of the A32. As a Starcraft pilot,

Daeson's skills were superb, and he had hoped his mastery would continue with the deployment of the machine's weaponry, but alas it was not to be. He struggled. It was everything he could do just to avoid being eliminated from his training. He assimilated all of the knowledge, but the focus required to implement and execute that knowledge eluded him. It was as if his hands and his head were out of sync. Linden, on the other hand, seemed to excel and missed no opportunity to gloat about it.

In just a few days, Daeson had lost his friends, his skills, his future, and his past. But in the still of the night when sleep was not his companion and the turmoil of his life wrestled with him, his thoughts turned to Raviel. Was she just a girl who happened to be near when his life fell apart? Or were his growing feelings for her genuine? Seeing her on the flight line was difficult. It was as if a portion of his heart and his thoughts were lost to her each time he saw her. She seemed to handle their situation much better than he. In fact, she gave not the slightest hint of familiarity toward him—not a glance, not a smile, nothing.

Finally, when he thought they might be clear of the consequences of that treacherous night, he arranged to meet her on the ocean shore where she had first begun to enchant him. She coldly agreed.

That night he waited late into the hours past midnight, each passing minute shredding what remained of the one good thing left in his life. After two hours, he took a deep breath and then mounted his aerobike to return home. He took one last hopeful glance behind him and saw her slowly walking his way. He wanted to run to her but was so completely at a loss as to what she was thinking that he just dismounted and waited, wondering if his feelings for her were as unreciprocated as it appeared they might be.

In the final ten paces that remained between them, Raviel hesitated before running and throwing her arms around his neck. Daeson held her quietly, letting the moment heal him. He lowered his head into the softness of her hair and felt restored.

"I've missed you," he said quietly into her ear.

Raviel nodded. He knew she was struggling with this forbidden relationship. She seemed almost too afraid to speak.

He held her until he felt her relax and then let go. She backed away and immediately turned to look at the ocean, not daring to look into his eyes.

"This can't happen," she said. "You know it can't."

"Why not?" He reached for her hand.

She watched his hand lift hers, waited, and then pulled back and walked away.

"Because of a million reasons...and because you don't really know me."

"I don't care how many reasons there are *against* it; I only need one *for* it."

Raviel turned back and stared at him. Her eyes were hard to read in the darkness.

"Don't you see how impossible this is? The Elite would never allow you and me to be together...never! We would be outcasts in both classes. What would we do? Sneak away once every few weeks to be together? To what end?"

Daeson slowly nodded. "You're right."

She seemed both justified and saddened by his acknowledgment.

"So instead, we leave it all behind. Come away with me, and we will build a life together as farmers in some remote region of Jypton. You and me—away from both Drudge and Elite."

"You speak nonsense!" Raviel said. She looked stunned by the suggestion. She motioned toward him. "You? A farmer! And me...," she stated as she shook her head. "I can't!"

Raviel seemed terrified by the thought of it. Daeson took a deep breath.

"I care for you, Raviel...and my life is unraveling around me."

Raviel's eyes softened.

Daeson motioned toward a large outcropping of rocks further down the shore. "How about we just sit and talk. I want to be near you and not pretend that I don't know you, just for a little while."

Raviel nodded. Daeson led her down the sandy shore toward the outcropping, where they sat and absorbed the cool night air and its soothing sounds. Anxious thoughts melted away as they laid back to gaze upward. Daeson reached for Raviel's hand, and she allowed it. He closed his eyes and cherished the warmth of her hand in his. This simple touch soothed him in a way that nothing else could. He thought of the twist of events that had caused his and Raviel's paths to cross, and at each crossing his heart became less and less his own. He smiled inwardly as he thought of the dance.

"When we danced, I saw a mark on your shoulder."

Raviel glanced over at him, her eyes once more fueling the flame of his heart.

"It is the mark of Ell Yon and of my clan. Every Raylean wears such a mark, signifying to which clan he or she belongs. Mine is the mark of the Jahrim Clan, the same clan to which you belong."

Daeson broke from her gaze and looked up into the night, thinking about what she had said. The brilliance of a trillion stars lit up the night sky in a beautiful display of eternity. The faint glow of the Aurora galaxy cloaked the night across the western sky. He shook his head.

"I have no clan...no family," he said.

Raviel held his hand a little tighter, turning her gaze to the stars too.

"What's it like up there?" she asked.

Daeson couldn't help the subtle smile that crossed his lips. That didn't happen much anymore.

"When I was just a lad, I used to climb to the top of the palace tower and lay on my back just as we are now, aching to touch them. Somehow I felt closer up there."

Raviel looked over at him. "So did I." She chuckled. "Minus the palace."

Daeson turned his head toward her. Even now her eyes were so full of life...so captivating. He'd rather look at her than the stars.

"What's it like?" Daeson repeated. "It's better...and worse. Beautiful and horrible. Peaceful and frightening. Wonderful and terrible. It's everything you've imagined and more."

Raviel looked back to the heavens.

"Something about the stars is calling me. We were once star travelers...the Rayleans." Raviel seemed lost in the glory of an ancient past.

"Really?" Daeson asked. All he could ever imagine the Rayleans being were the servants of Jypton.

Raviel pointed. "See there?"

Daeson leaned closer to her to follow the aim of her index finger.

"Yes, the Omega Nebula," he said. He didn't move away.

"Uh-huh. Thousands of years ago that was our beginning. When the Omega sun went supernova, our home world was destroyed. As you know, even to this day that region of space is uninhabitable because of the Omegeon radiation."

"Yes," Daeson interrupted. "In our Astro class, they taught us that the Omegeon particle emitted from the nebula is deadly to all living things even in small doses."

Raviel continued. "After the supernova, our legends tell of a mighty people that travelled from system to system, trading and gathering resources. Although we had no home world, we grew strong. Many planets feared us, but we honored those who honored us. With no planet to call our own, our home was our bond with each other. In that day we were one clan...the clan of Tobias Rayl, the one through whom Sovereign Ell Yon chose to establish his people and give his promise."

"You say 'we'...you make it sound as if it happened yesterday," Daeson said.

"Our people have a bond with each other that is timeless. I consider my ancestors of ten thousand years ago as important to my future as my grandparents. We have been preserved by Sovereign Ell Yon throughout the ages."

Daeson looked back to the stars. "Ell Yon...I keep hearing you and your people talk about this mystical figure."

Now it was Raviel who turned to look at Daeson.

"Not mystical. He is powerful and intelligent, but more than that, he is good. There is no evil in him."

"You make him sound invincible," Daeson said. "I find it difficult to believe someone like that is real, and if he is, that he could be that perfect."

"It's because you don't yet understand who he is," Raviel replied.

"And how can you? You say no one has seen him for thousands of years, yet you and the rest of the Rayleans place all of your hope on him. Seems extremely dubious."

Raviel frowned. She even looked hurt, as if he had insulted her personally. He didn't like the thought of offending her. Time to change the subject.

"It's strange. We are never taught about the history of the Rayleans. How did they...*we* end up as servants to the Jyptonians?" he asked.

Raviel looked over at him with eyes renewed. His change of pronoun seemed to delight her.

"Jypton was the wealthiest and most powerful planet in this sector of the galaxy. They welcomed our people with open arms. After centuries of wandering, the people of Rayl found comfort and peace here. Over time our ships became derelicts, and the people became too comfortable. That's when the Jyptonians became our masters. We had become dependent on them, and they had become dependent on us...or at least our labor. Our technology skills became something the Jyptonians couldn't live without, yet they were unwilling to yield any authority. We became indentured servants, along with all of its ugly effects. This has been our culture for over twelve hundred years."

Raviel closed her eyes. "Even if by some miracle we were able to free ourselves from the Jyptonians, there is no one to lead us...to show us how to govern ourselves. We've been conditioned to serve...not lead."

Daeson rose up on one elbow and looked at her.

"So this is your welcome to the Raylean race?" Daeson quipped. "I'm so encouraged and grateful to be a part of such a sad future with you."

Raviel laughed and squeezed his hand again.

"There is an ancient prophecy of an oracle that one day a leader will come and save us."

"Save you from the Jyptonians?" Daeson asked.

Raviel smiled. "No...from Deitum Prime and from the curse it brings to the galaxy...and from the Scourge. It will be the great Day of Reclamation."

"Hmm," was all that Daeson responded with. He just couldn't seem to understand why the Rayleans were so against Deitum Prime. It offered so much. Raviel sat up and leaned on one outstretched arm, which put her looking down on Daeson. Her dark brown hair hung down, and she pushed it over her right ear and shoulder so she could see Daeson clearly. A subtle and curious smile crossed her lips.

"Would you like to be reclaimed?"

Daeson's heart quickened. He wasn't sure what it meant, but how could he deny her?

"Reclaimed? What does that mean?" he asked.

Raviel's smiled broadened. She jumped from the rock and ran toward the bluffs that separated the sand of the beach from the grassy plains nearby. Daeson sat up and watched as she disappeared into the tall grass and reappeared just moments later. She was carrying something in her hand. Soon she was sitting once more with Daeson, face to face.

"Do you know what these are?" Raviel asked, holding out her hand. She offered two palm-sized bright red flowers.

"Some sort of wild flower." Daeson responded.

"These are Wild Crimson Roses. They're not indigenous to Jypton."

"But I've seen them everywhere," Daeson said.

Raviel set one flower on her lap and slowly began pulling the petals off of the other. Something inside of Daeson hurt to see her destroy the perfect beauty of the rose.

Raviel become quiet...respectful...as each of the seven perfect petals was parted from the stem.

"Why did you do that?" Daeson asked, lifting the other flower from her lap.

"For anything to be reclaimed, it requires the sacrifice of the perfect, the innocent, and the beautiful."

Daeson looked up from the rose in his hand to see Raviel ceremoniously layer each of the seven petals on top of each other.

"The Rayleans brought the Crimson Rose with us because of our custom of reclamation."

She looked up at Daeson. "It's a sacred thing to us."

Daeson nodded, but he didn't understand.

Raviel reached for Daeson's hand and opened up his palm. She then took the stack of rose petals and began twisting them until a single red drop of the flower's fluid fell to his palm. She then dipped her finger into the blood-red liquid and gently swiped it across his forehead just above his brows, finishing the ritual with two smaller swipes down each side of his temples. Daeson imagined that he looked quite silly with the red dye all over his face, but Raviel didn't laugh.

"It is believed that the Crimson Rose holds trace amounts of Omeganite in its petals. The Omeganite is the only substance in the galaxy that can destroy Deitum Prime."

Daeson pursed his lips. "Okay, but I don't feel any different. Is this it?"

Raviel smiled. "It is more symbolic of our hope for a future reclamation. But no, that's not it...now it must be sealed."

Daeson tilted his head to the side, wondering what that meant. Raviel then leaned forward and kissed his forehead. Her warm lips sent tingles across his brow and down his temples. He smiled.

"Well, that was nice, but I'm not so sure my Deitum Prime levels have been diminished much, especially since I took supplements of it this morning."

Raviel sat back and shook her head. "At least I tried. Perhaps someday you'll understand."

Daeson reached up and touched her cheek. "I'm sorry. Please don't be disappointed...not with the short time we have left together."

Raviel forced a smile.

"My turn," Daeson said and then repeated the ritual for Raviel. He was somewhat amazed when he swiped the bright red fluid above her brow and down her temples. She nearly glowed in the night because of it.

The reclamation ritual was a reprieve from the woes of their predicament, and for a few short hours, the soothing sounds of the ocean helped wash away the pain of reality for both of them. Their goodbye that night was long and difficult. It might be weeks before they would see each other again.

Raviel rode the grav-rail back home in numbed silence. The Council of the Plexus would be pleased. She had dared to tell them of Lockridge's growing feelings for her, and they had encouraged her to use that to their advantage.

"When feelings are involved, especially feelings of love, there is no limit to the information you may gain access to," the Council Lead had said. His eyes narrowed. "I don't need to remind you of the importance of your mission. You are as close as we have ever been to the royal family and its power. Regardless of his origins, he has been raised a Jyptonian, and his loyalties will be to them. Be certain that you keep your head, Agent Arko. Can you do that?"

Raviel straightened. "Of course. I understand."

Raviel's own words echoed in her mind. Could she keep her head? She felt like a traitor to both causes. In the world of secret agents, there was no safe ground...no room to walk the fence. She had to choose to whom she would be loyal, and the choice was obvious.

CHAPTER

9

Plexus Agent

The end of Daeson's training in the A32 was near, paltry as it was. He felt as though its mastery was ever out of reach, as if he were trying to lay hold of the morning mist rising from the Aqua Gardens on the palace grounds. It was a depressing way to finish up his academy training—from top of the class to barely graduating.

Today he had no flights scheduled, only two academic classes, a lab, and a sim ride. As he walked toward his astro-lab, he was intercepted.

"Master Lockridge," a voice called out from behind him.

Daeson turned to see Tig approaching. He hadn't talked to the cadet since the week he had rescued him from a fiery reentry.

Tig was carrying his flight gear. He was ready to fly a mission.

"Cadet Tig...good to see you."

"And you, my lord." Tig offered the customary head bow when addressing a governing Elite, even if Daeson was a fellow cadet. The solemn approach by Tig could have been interpreted as reasonable respect by a man of lower estate, but Daeson suspected something more. Tig quickly glanced left then right, confirming Daeson's suspicion.

"What's on your mind?" Daeson asked.

Tig's eyes narrowed.

"My father is a lieutenant in the Sentry Force, responsible for security in Drudgetown."

Daeson's heart nearly stopped. All of the faded fear of that fateful night rose up again and began to choke him. He tried to look calm.

"Okay," he prompted.

Tig looked around again. "You must keep this confidential, my lord."

Daeson put a hand on Tig's shoulder and pulled him into a walkway. "You have my word. What's going on? What have you heard?"

Tig looked at Daeson, creases across his forehead.

"I overheard my father communicating with the captain. Today they plan to arrest the mechtech that works on your Starcraft. And..."

Raviel!

"And what?" Daeson urged.

"My father says they think you are involved with her in some way." Tig looked Daeson in the eye. "What would you like me to do?" he asked.

Tig's words sounded distant and hollow as Daeson's mind began to race with a thousand thoughts, all leading to irrecoverable disaster. His hand slowly dropped from Tig's shoulder. The one thought that screamed the loudest was the one that screamed *save her!*

He turned toward the direction of the hangar, but Tig grabbed his arm.

"What are you going to do?" Tig asked.

Daeson looked down at Tig's hand and then up at the Colloquial, but Tig didn't flinch.

"It's too late to warn her. The sentries are already entering the hangar."

Daeson's stupor turned to anger. He jerked his arm away from Tig's grasp. "I have to do something!" Daeson said through clenched teeth.

"You do have feelings for her then," Tig said bluntly. That revelation shattered any ambivalence left in Daeson's heart. "How much are you willing to do?"

The question put Daeson on his heels.

"What do you mean?" Daeson asked, his eyes narrowing.

Tig hesitated. "The life of a Drudge means nothing to them. And if there are others involved in the murder of the sentry, they'll not stop until they get the information out of her." Tig looked down at the ground and then back at Daeson. "She won't survive."

Daeson became instantly nauseated. He turned away and ran his hand through his hair and down the back of his neck. Then he looked back at Tig.

He considered the possibility of using his influence as a member of the royal family to set her free, but it would raise too many questions, especially if they really did think he was involved with her in some way. The Chancellor and Linden in particular would not stop until they found out why.

"I have to go to her," Daeson said.

He turned and ran to the hangar, hoping against hope that by some miracle he would be in time to warn Raviel. Fear strangled him. This was his fault. Whatever was going to happen to her was his and his alone to bear. He had promised to protect her. He was trying to formulate a plan as he went, resolving in his heart to do whatever it took to save her.

Upon entering the hangar, there was no question about his timing. Sentries were everywhere, and the commotion near his Starcraft was unmistakably the focus of all of the attention. He broke through a line of mechtechs, student pilots, and instructors to see Raviel face down on the pavement near his Starcraft. One sentry had his knee in her back, while locking her wrists into composite fetters. She looked up at him, cheek bleeding and bruised. Daeson pushed forward, but two sentries restrained him from coming closer.

"What's this all about?" Daeson demanded, doing his best to feign authority and consternation.

"Ah, Daeson...come," Daeson turned to his left and saw Linden motioning for the sentries to let him through. Linden? But why?

"Lin...Prince Lockridge, what's going on?"

Daeson was confused. This arrest had to be about the murder of the sentry in Drudgetown, and Linden wouldn't normally concern himself with such an affair. Of course he had significant power and authority as the heir apparent to the throne of Jypton, but that was deferred until he was finished with the academy, or so Daeson thought.

"What we have here," Linden motioned toward Raviel, "is a case of discovering a true enemy to the peace and prosperity of Jypton."

Two sentries lifted Raviel to her feet. Daeson trembled. To see her like this was unbearable. Perhaps if he confessed, Linden would let her go. After all, he was the guilty one—not her. It would be the end of him, but it was his only play. Raviel glared at Linden and then turned her gaze to Daeson. Contempt spilled from her eyes. Loathing fury filled her countenance. He could hardly believe it was the same face that had enraptured him not too long ago.

"You recognize the Drudge, don't you?" Linden asked. He walked closer to her and leaned to within inches of her face. Then he turned and looked at Daeson. *What was he doing? Did he know? Why was he even involved?*

"Yes, of course. She is the mechtech for my Starcraft."

Linden smiled. "Oh, she is more than that, cousin. Much, much more."

Daeson could hardly think straight. Surely Linden was playing with him. He glanced at Raviel and saw fear masked by the contempt she was displaying, and it pierced his heart through.

"We have discovered that she is connected to the murder of a sentry in Drudgetown and —"

"Linden, I—" Daeson stepped closer.

"You live in your ivory towers and pretend to offer justice and peace!" Raviel shouted. "Your hands are red with the blood of thousands of innocent Rayleans!" One of the sentries struck her, and her head jolted from the impact. Her lip spilled more blood and swelled instantly.

"There it is," Linden said. "My suspicions confirmed."

Daeson looked away. "What do you mean? Why are *you* involved?"

Linden stood between him and Raviel. He looked Daeson in the eyes. "I am here because my father has assigned me to lead the task force to discover who belongs to the Plexus."

"Plexus?" Daeson asked. Linden continued to stare at him and then tilted his head.

"The Plexus is a Drudge network of trained spies intent on subverting the Jyptonian government and in particular the royal family. Because we are cadets here, we knew the academy was a target." Linden smiled again and pointed at Raviel. "She's a spy, Daeson, and she's been using you to feed information to the Plexus."

Daeson slowly turned his gaze toward Raviel. She was still recovering from the strike of the sentry. Could this be true? He walked to Raviel...the girl he thought he cared for. Was he just a target...a pawn of hers? A pawn to reach the royal family? The mounting betrayal in the pit of his stomach began to ravage his soul.

He glared down at her. "Is this true, Drudge...are you a spy?"

Raviel looked up at Daeson, and for one fraction of a moment, her eyes softened before turning hard with rebellion.

"And the fury of Ell Yon shall fall upon the enemies of Rayl, and they shall be utterly destroyed from the four corners of the galaxy."

Words of an ancient oracle were spoken with such boldness, yet woven into each syllable was a silent plea. But the only message Daeson heard was contemptible betrayal. The words shattered the last of his hope for anything good in his life.

"Take her away and prepare her for Major Kordo," Linden ordered.

Two sentries gruffly whisked her away, while the other sentries dispersed those gathered to see the spectacle.

"What will happen to her?" Daeson asked, his voice somber but steady. His eyes were locked on the prisoner who had stolen his heart...the girl who knew his secret. How much time did he have? Would it be the first information she would divulge? That Master Daeson Lockridge was Raylean, a mere Drudge living in the court of the royal family? Then a horrid thought hit him—would they suspect *him* to be a spy?

"We will extract the information we need from her, and then she will be executed." Linden's voice was cold. "She will be a key factor in discovering, dismantling, and destroying the Plexus. We knew their network was extensive...perhaps even global, but we could never find them. She's the first real break our government has had in many years. Father will be pleased."

Daeson looked over at Linden and forced a smile. "Well done, Linden. She was right under my nose, and I had no idea."

Linden returned a smug smile.

"Kordo is going to want to talk to you too. We need to know if anything was compromised."

Daeson nodded. "Of course, but you need not be concerned."

Linden glared at Daeson. "I'm sure of that." He turned to walk away.

"Linden," Daeson called.

Linden turned part way and gave Daeson a sideways glance. "I have a flight to brief. What do you want?"

"How long have you suspected her?"

"A while."

Daeson sneered. "Why didn't you tell me? I could've..." Daeson stopped as understanding dawned on him. "You were using me...using me to get to her."

Linden fully turned to face Daeson. "She was using *you* to get to *me*. Perhaps you should be more careful in the future about who you keep company with, cousin. Your privilege as a distant member of the royal family will only go so far."

Linden glared at Daeson. The fruit of jealousy had fully ripened. As Linden's power and authority had increased, his heart had hardened, and Daeson knew their friendship was truly at its end.

"I understand," Daeson replied.

Linden continued to stare. "Do you?"

He didn't wait for an answer. He turned and walked away, as if he ruled the planet...and soon he would.

Raviel set her face like stone, but on the inside she was terrified. No, it was much worse than that. No word aptly described the depth of fear that was devouring her soul. These brutes were taking her to be tortured and then executed. She had known from the first day of her training that this was a possibility. Compounding the horror that awaited her was the knowledge that the lives of many others would depend on her strength to endure the pain to come. Could she bear it? She knew the answer. She'd heard stories. The gritty and dark face of Jypton was reserved for people like her—rebels. No one survived it. Everyone talked. Death was the reward that prisoners pleaded for. If only she'd not let Lockridge tease her heart so!

He seemed to genuinely care for her, and she couldn't deny the struggle of her own feelings. She had convinced herself that it had all been for the sake of information...for her job as a spy for the Plexus, but deep down it was real, and she knew it. The pain of betrayal on his face was hard to see. She wanted to explain, but that would never happen. Instead she chose to play out her role as the cold-hearted spy she had been trained to be. Perhaps if she performed well enough, he would be spared to some degree.

Four sentries escorted her to the prisoner transport vehicle. Two of them mounted sentry aerobikes, while the other two searched her and threw her into the back chamber. With her hands secured tightly behind her, she landed on her shoulder and face. Pain shot down her arm and around to her back...it was just the beginning. She heard the sentries close and lock the hatch.

Raviel lay still for a few seconds, waiting for the pain to abate before she rolled to a sitting position and leaned against the chamber wall. She felt the transport lift off to its hover position and then looked at the locked hatch, wishing desperately that it would never open. She began to question whether anything she had done had actually helped her people. Had she given the Plexus any valuable information at all? Or was she a terrible liability that would undo everything they had been working for the past one hundred years? She needed to know her life would count for something, but at this moment in time, despair was her only companion.

She thought of Daeson and dared to let her heart dream of a different outcome. What could it hurt now? What value was there in protecting her heart when it would soon stop beating altogether? But the pleasant thoughts could not be maintained, for within seconds the crushing weight of reality destroyed them, and stark fear welled up so strong she found it difficult to breathe. The minutes ticked by. The sentry security facility could not be far away now.

"Sovereign Ell Yon, your might and wisdom are vast...do you see me? Can you help me? Will you help me? Please!"

CHAPTER

10

No Return

Slipstream Conduit – a space pathway connecting two large bodies of mass, typically planets, which allow traversing large distances by circumventing the time dilation effect of light speed travel. A space craft must be equipped with a jump drive engine to utilize a slipstream conduit.

Daeson stood still amidst the dissipating chaos of the hangar. The scene held him hostage, like a bad dream from which he could not awaken.

"She will die." Tig's quiet voice came from behind Daeson.

Daeson slowly turned to face him. "And if what Prince Lockridge says about her is true? If she is a spy for the Plexus?"

Tig's face was expressionless. "She will die," he simply repeated.

Daeson closed his eyes. Something deep inside him pushed back against the betrayal that was scarring his heart. *Let her die! Let the betraying Drudge spy die!*

Thoughts he hated but could not deny vied for his logical response.

He took two steps away from Tig and stared at the dark and murky sky just beyond the massive hangar doors. If he did nothing...if Raviel was executed for a crime he committed, regardless of whether she was a spy or not, it would haunt him for the rest of his life. He forcibly silenced the thoughts he knew were not his own, turned, and came back to Tig, eyes narrow and hard. "You said you would be my ally."

"I did, and my word is my honor."

"Then help me save her," Daeson petitioned.

Tig shook his head. "How? I've been to the security facility. Once inside, there is no return. Their security is impenetrable."

Daeson thought for a moment and then looked directly at Tig. "I need a Starcraft, and I need it now."

Daeson's window of opportunity to reach Raviel before she entered the Security Force facility was narrow, and Tig was the only one that could help him.

Tig's eyes lit up. "I'm scheduled for a solo flight in...." He looked at his timepiece before finishing his thought, "twenty minutes." He nodded toward the cadets' flight dressing room.

Daeson and Tig walked briskly in that direction, talking in hushed tones as they went.

"How long will it take the sentries to transport her to the security facility?"

Tig thought for a moment. "Once they leave the academy, you'll have about twenty-five minutes."

Daeson nodded. "That's cutting it close."

They arrived at the flight room—it was empty. Daeson looked at Tig, knowing that Tig was putting himself at grave risk to help Daeson. Tig seemed to sense his gratitude. "I just have to know—are you doing this to save her or to save yourself?"

The question hit Daeson square in the chest. It offended and exposed him.

"Both," he responded.

Tig nodded, handed his gear over to Daeson, peeled off his nametag, and stuck it on Daeson's flight suit.

Daeson looked down at the nametag and then up at Tig. "Why are you helping me, Tig?"

Tig hesitated, looking as if he were searching Daeson's eyes for assurance that he would be safe with the words that would follow. He lowered his head.

"My father has served with the Sentry Force for over twenty-five years. During his first few years, he patrolled Drudgetown every night."

Tig looked up. Daeson couldn't begin to imagine why this had anything to do with his willingness to help him. He nodded, encouraging Tig to continue.

"One night there was an uprising, and my father was called in with a dozen other sentries to subdue the Drudge rebels. They did, and most of the rebels were killed, but during the exchange, my father accidently wounded a young woman who was caught in the crossfire. As she lay bleeding in the street, my father came to help her. The other sentries told him to leave her, but he could not."

Tig stopped. "He's a good man, my father."

"What happened to the young woman?" Daeson asked.

"My father helped her, and they fell in love."

Daeson cocked his head, a little stunned. "You're..."

Tig nodded. "Yes. I'm half Raylean."

"Your mother?"

Tig looked away. His gaze grew hard.

"They hid their love for each other as long as they could. A Raylean oracle secretly performed the bonding ceremony for them. They knew they could never be together, but they found happiness in the time they had."

Daeson felt the sadness coming.

"Had?"

Tig looked back at Daeson, eyes wet. He shook his head.

"I never knew her. Shortly after I was born." Tig's voice grew cold and hard. "She was killed in a raid on Drudgetown...by a sentry. My father took me and raised me on his own." Tig took a deep breath. "My father and I are caught in between worlds. The injustice...I thought that perhaps as a Starcraft pilot I could one day make a difference, even if in a small way."

Tig looked at Daeson with eyes of steely resolve. "I think that day has come."

Daeson stared at this courageous man. Was it purely fate that had caused him to save Tig that day weeks ago? Something told Daeson it was much more than that.

"Make it a good one," Tig said, steeling himself.

"Sorry about this," Daeson said and then punched him across his left cheekbone.

Tig recovered and winced from the pain. "I'll try to stay out of sight as long as possible."

Daeson nodded, put on his helmet, and went to steal a Starcraft.

Once he arrived at the Starcraft, Daeson pushed the ground crew to hurry his launch and then departed on the expected flight plan. He cleared the city, dropped low to the horizon, and doubled back. Flying straight to the sentry's security facility, he traced the route back to the academy. Just a short distance from the facility, he spotted the prisoner transport vehicle. His next action would end his life on Jypton as he knew it. What if he were risking everything for a woman who was a cold-hearted spy and was simply playing his emotions to gain information? Every logical and reasonable thought told him to stop. He had a few more seconds. He could still turn back.

Don't be a fool! Save yourself! Think of what you could accomplish as a ruler on Jypton! Let her die!

Just as he was about to turn back, the image of Raviel running to embrace him saturated his mind. Was she just acting? Was she really that good? The few tender moments they had shared together seemed so real. He had to know. The thought of abandoning her was too much, and it pushed him forward.

Two escort sentries on aerobikes led the transport vehicle through a crowded section of the city. He would have to surgically remove Raviel as quickly as possible, and he had to make sure no communication escaped to give him away. He set his phaser burst gun at the lowest setting for broad field dispersion, hoping it would stun and not kill the escorts. The secure chamber of the prisoner transport vehicle would offer Raviel the greatest protection from his shot. Executing a quartering tactical approach between two large buildings to minimize his exposure, he targeted the convoy and fired his phaser array. The escorts and twenty other vehicles immediately careened out of control as their drivers fell unconscious from the shot. Daeson flipped on his communications jammer and targeted the transport vehicle with his grappler field. He felt the Starcraft lurch from the invisible tether. It was then that he realized that every action he had taken in the last sixty seconds had been executed with perfect precision and skill. Unlike the last few months, everything fell in sync at once, and it felt good.

He wasted no time in pushing up his thrusters until both he and the transport lifted from the wreckage out of the chaos below. Daeson flew as fast as he dared, skimming the tops of buildings. The dangling transport was an odd sight indeed. Once beyond the city, he accelerated further to ensure he would have enough time to extract Raviel and return back to the Starcraft before the sentries could find them. Not certain as to how effective the phaser array might have been on the sentries in the transport, he found a ravine to wedge the vehicle in, thus prohibiting the sentries from exiting through their side access doors.

As Daeson disengaged the grappling field and quickly landed the Starcraft, heavy clouds began to spill their watery contents. Daeson jumped from the cockpit and climbed down the ravine to the back of the transport. He wiped water from his eyes before he fired his Talon at the locking mechanism on the door. Upon opening the door, he saw Raviel lying on the floor bruised and bleeding, but alive. Her eyes widened at the sight of him, and he wasn't sure how to respond.

"Daeson!" she gasped, her voice trembling with fear and relief.

Approaching her carefully, he rolled her on her stomach and extended his Talon part way, using the stasis field of the knife blade to cut through the fetters. Once free, she rose up and flung her arms around his neck, but he didn't return the embrace.

"We must move quickly," he said coldly.

Raviel slowly let loose of him and lowered her head. At that moment, he knew it was all true. She *was* a spy and had betrayed him. He had risked everything for one who had been trying to destroy him from the onset.

He turned and exited the transport. As he climbed up the ravine, his anger swelled, and he had a mind to leave her out in the wilderness. He could hear her climbing the ravine behind him, struggling because of the fresh mud created by the storm overhead.

"Daeson...please let me explain," she pleaded between breaths.

More lies, he thought. He reached the top of the ravine and marched to the Starcraft.

Raviel clambered over the edge of the ravine and ran to him, pulling him down from the first step of the Starcraft ladder.

"Let me explain!" she shouted over a clap of thunder.

Daeson glared at her. "Explain what? That this was all just a ruse so you could plot a way to kill Linden and me? That you used me to destroy myself?"

He turned his back and reached for the ladder, but this time Raviel grabbed him and used a move from her training to sweep his feet and put him on the muddy ground. Daeson looked up at her, stunned at how quickly she had taken him down. She put her hands on her hips.

"I'm going to expl—"

Her words were cut short as Daeson kicked her feet out to put her down and then rolled on top of her, grabbing her arms and pinning them against the ground. He scowled. "Lies!" he shouted at her over the sounds of the storm swelling around them.

Rain pelted her face as she shook her head. "No." she said, her jaw clenched.

Daeson stood up and walked away as Raviel recovered her feet. He came back and pointed a finger at her. "I cared for you! You lied to me!" He clenched his fists. "You...betrayed me, Raviel. Or is that even your name?"

Raviel lifted her chin, defying his accusations. "I never lied to you, Daeson. It is true that I am a spy for the Plexus, but I never planned on—" She looked away and then back into his eyes. "You...you changed everything."

Her words softened Daeson. Even now, how was it that she could have any influence over him? And yet, it was there. He steeled his heart against it.

"I don't believe you! Why should I believe you?" He yelled, fury pouring out with each word. He went back to the ladder and set his foot on the first rung again. He could hear the faint shouts and pounding from the transport in the ravine below them. By now they had made communication with sentry headquarters. He hesitated.

"I don't blame you for hating me. I wanted to tell you...I tried to tell you." With each word, Raviel's voice deepened with sorrow. He could feel her tears spilling over his heart. "I resolved to complete my mission no matter what, and then when you told me you were one of us...a Raylean, I couldn't stop from caring for you. I didn't want to hurt you."

Daeson turned his head to look at her out of the corner of his eye. Water dripped down his head and from his eyelids. How could he dare care for her?

"I'm sorry. Please believe me."

Daeson turned around to see the battered, muddy face of the girl who had stolen his heart. She was tough, yet tender. Clearly she was exactly who Linden claimed she was...a highly trained underground spy of the Plexus. But was she more? Thunder clapped and lightning flashed above as the rain continued to drench them. Raviel took one step toward Daeson. If he left her here, she was still as good as dead. She knew that. Was he being played again just so she could survive? How could he possibly know?

"You came for me." Her words were barely audible. She glanced down at the prisoner transport and then back at Daeson. "You can still save yourself. Go."

Daeson continued to glare at her, his despair complete. He shook his head and stepped aside. "We must go," he stated in a matter-of-fact tone. She stepped to the ladder and then turned and kissed him on the cheek.

"Will you betray me with a kiss?" he asked, fighting the anger that still lingered.

"I will never betray you," she declared before climbing the ladder and jumping into the second cockpit seat.

Daeson helped her strap into the seat. When he stole a quick glance her direction, he noticed that she had never taken her eyes off his face. There would be much to forgive—perhaps too much. But for the sake of his own conscience, he would save her and then be done with her.

"This could get violent. Better hang on," he instructed as he checked her harness and handed her the helmet for the second cockpit before quickly strapping himself into the front cockpit.

Before the canopy was fully closed, they were lifting and accelerating up and away from the place that would soon be overrun with sentries. Pursuit was imminent, so he set a course away from Athlone and toward the barren lands.

Daeson heard the click of Raviel's mic through his head set. "Daeson, we have to go back to the academy."

"Are you mad? Absolutely not!"

"If Linden's people recover my data logs, many innocent Rayleans will die," Raviel pleaded.

"You mean Rayleans that are plotting a revolt against my family? *Those* innocent people?"

Daeson heard Raviel click the mic, but she said nothing for a few seconds.

"They're not your family, Daeson. And had the Chancellor been successful twenty-two years ago, you wouldn't be alive today," Raviel replied.

The image of his mother sharing the truth of his origin filled his mind once more...the moment his life morphed into some strange story.

"These people...your people have endured the pain you are feeling for generations. And now there are a few who have the courage to try to change this torment. Those are the people that will die...those are the people I must safeguard. Please...I must try."

Daeson could hardly contain his anger.

"They will find you, and they will kill you," he said coldly. "They are probably combing through your belongings right now."

"Perhaps, but my logs are hidden in a different location. I couldn't live with myself if I didn't try...if I just let them die."

She spoke the same words he had thought himself when considering whether or not to rescue her. He shook his head. Her courage was remarkable...it was hard not to admire.

He banked the Starcraft ninety degrees and pulled hard on the stick until the nose of the mighty craft was pointed on a course directly to the academy.

"It's been twelve minutes since I attacked your transport. We will be at the academy in three. The sentry force will first contact the Jypton Planetary Aero Force. Once they've reviewed any data, alerts will spread from there. If we're lucky, we may have ten minutes tops before every sentry and Aero Force ship on the planet will be looking for us."

"I understand," Raviel replied.

Daeson clenched his teeth. This was suicide.

"Our best bet is to land in an open bay in C Flight," Raviel said. "They are on a night schedule this week, so there shouldn't be any mechtechs or ground crews there."

"Can you get to your logs and be back in six minutes?" Daeson asked.

"Yes. It'll be close, but I can do it."

"If I see *any* indication they are on to us, I'm aborting, and we are out of there. Do you understand?"

"I understand." Her mic didn't release. "Thank you."

Daeson said nothing in return. He had just awakened a sleeping dragon and was now flying right back into its jaws. He had to be absolutely out of his mind.

He approached the academy as fast as possible without drawing attention. The radio communication with control seemed normal so far, but it didn't ease the extreme tension Daeson was feeling. He flew his Starcraft through the massive hangar doors and set her down in an empty C-Flight bay, bringing the engines to idle but keeping them running. He flipped the switch to open the canopy. Thankfully no personnel were nearby. Two rows over, he could see ground crews readying to launch a flight of Starcrafts , but they seemed too occupied with their duties to notice.

The canopy was mostly open.

"Go!" he ordered.

As Raviel scurried down the extending ladder, he leaned over the side. "If you see anyone or hear an alert, you get back here immediately—log or no log. Is that clear?"

Raviel jumped from the ladder and lifted a thumb in the air as she bolted across the hangar floor toward her mechtech facility. On the far side of the hangar, she disappeared through a doorway and down a corridor. The next few moments were agonizing for Daeson. He unholstered his Talon as a precaution and waited. One minute. The seconds slowly ticked by. He monitored radio channels looking for alerts...all clear. Two minutes. A flight of four Starcrafts launched on a training mission. Three minutes.

"Come on, Raviel," he pleaded quietly.

Four minutes.

Daeson kept his eyes locked on the corridor doorway that Raviel had entered. Still nothing.

Five minutes.

Daeson's heart was now racing. Sweat began to trickle down his sides, and his legs hurt from the adrenalin. Just as the doorway to the corridor burst open, a siren rang out that rattled Daeson to the bone. Raviel sprinted toward the Starcraft, a satchel on her back. Close behind her was an academy guard. In spite of her head start and speed, Daeson realized she would never make it.

Halfway across the hangar floor, the guard stopped and aimed his Talon at her. Before he could get a shot off, Daeson took aim and fired. His shot passed just over Raviel's head and impacted the concrete at the feet of the guard. It bought her a few more seconds as the guard recovered and took aim at Daeson instead. Multiple shots were exchanged before the guard realized that Raviel should be his primary target. He aimed at her and shot, but it went wide, impacting the left wing of the Starcraft.

Daeson gave Raviel four more bursts of cover fire, but just as she reached the base of the Starcraft, she diverted toward a mechtech cart to grab a flight processor interface module. Daeson nearly cursed. He continued to fire cover rounds as Raviel made her way back to the ladder. She scurried up and dove into the cockpit. At that, the guard unleashed a volley of shots aimed at the engine of the Starcraft, but Daeson had already flipped on the E-shield once Raviel was inside.

The field instantly dissipated the guard's shots, and the canopy came down as Daeson lifted the Starcraft out of its hangar bay and spun about 180°, immediately accelerating toward the massive hangar doors. Sirens continued to blare the alert to the entire academy.

"The doors are closing," Raviel said through heavy breaths.

"Strap in!" he shouted back.

He pushed the throttles to 50%, accelerating far beyond a safe speed inside the hangar. It was obvious the Starcraft's wingspan would not clear the doors. He flipped the master arm on to charge his plasma cannon, but there wouldn't be enough time. Rolling the Starcraft 90°, he lifted the nose to maintain horizontal flight. Two seconds later they screamed through the remaining narrow slit of the hangar doors. He heard Raviel sigh.

"That was close. Now where?" she asked through the com link.

"I'm still working on that part."

He accelerated to full speed, flying as close to the city contour as possible and leaving a wake of broken glass in the buildings behind him. Once they cleared the city, he dropped low to hug the terrain.

"Every Aero Force Starcraft on alert is looking for us by now. Can you disable the location transponder?" Daeson asked.

"Already working on it," Raviel replied.

The air around the Starcraft exploded in fire from a plasma cannon burst.

Daeson immediately pulled back on the stick, initiating a tight vertical loop so he could get eyes on his attacker. The g-forces hurt, and he heard Raviel groan under the pressure until the cockpit-compensating anti-gravity buffers engaged. He strained to look high over his head to get his eyes on the threat. Two A32s in loose formation were on his tail, but his quick response had negated their blind advantage. His targeting computer had already locked on to both Starcrafts.

"Stand down and return to base, Starcraft victor three niner."

Daeson recognized the voice of one of his instructors. Although this instructor had prior Aero Force experience, Daeson thought it unusual that they would allow an academy Starcraft flight to pursue him. Then he realized it was just to delay his escape. Daeson engaged, holding nothing back. He had seconds to turn his defensive position into an offensive one before the full power of the Planetary Aero Forces was on him.

"Hang on, Raviel. This is going to be brutal."

At the top of his loop, he briefly penetrated the cloud cover. He cut power to the engines, engaged the atmospheric speed brake, and initiated the nose vector thrusters. The maneuver had the effect of instantaneously spinning the Starcraft in place, which nearly tore the ship apart. For a few seconds they were flying backwards and falling. Now back below the cloud cover the nose of his Starcraft was pointed right at the other two Starcrafts. He simultaneously fired his plasma cannon at the lead ship, while pushing the throttles to full power to regain forward flight. The plasma burst tore right through the lead Starcraft's right engine, and the pilot ejected a few seconds later. Daeson closed in on the next Starcraft and quickly acquired a target lock.

"Daeson, don't!" Raviel's voice screamed through the com link.

"There's no going back now," Daeson said, his finger hovering over the fire button as he completed the last few degrees of the turn for a targeting computer solution.

"It's Prince Linden! I saw the flight schedule earlier today. According to the transponder, that's his Starcraft. Repercussions on the Rayleans would be global!"

The targeted Starcraft was diving and rolling down to the terrain for cover, but Daeson stayed with him. He recognized Linden's flying techniques. Daeson closed the distance on him while keeping a target lock. Linden tried a few more erratic maneuvers, but Daeson would not be shaken. Finally Linden's Starcraft quit maneuvering and flew straight and level.

Linden was taunting him now, daring him to pull the trigger. Daeson's finger rested on the fire button, his targeting computer locked and flashing red in anticipation of the kill. Seconds passed. He broke lock and accelerated until he was side by side with Linden. Flipping up his visor, he looked over at the man he had once called friend...cousin...brother. Linden lifted his visor and stared back at Daeson.

Raviel's voice broke in, her voice urgent. "I've got twelve Planetary Starcrafts coming our way. They'll be on us in less than sixty seconds."

The radio clicked. There was a pause and then, "If you do this, you're a dead man, Daeson. Land and I'll do everything I can to protect you."

"You would protect a lowly Drudge?" Daeson replied.

Silence. Had Linden known all along?

"Starcrafts closing in from the west," Raviel reported.

"Goodbye, Linden."

Daeson jammed the throttles full forward and pulled back on the stick to take the Starcraft pure vertical. The acceleration was nothing short of thrilling. He heard Raviel gasp. They pierced the thick clouds but just a few seconds later burst into the vibrant blue sky above.

"Where are we going?" she asked.

"Space...we've got to make it to one of the closest slipstream conduits."

"But won't they have Starcrafts guarding the entrances?" Raviel asked.

"Yes and we have to stay clear of any Aero Force destroyers. There's one conduit they won't be guarding though," Daeson stated as he plotted a course. "The Omega conduit."

"But what about the Omega Nebula's radiation on the other side? It will kill us!"

Daeson's sensor displayed a fleet of twelve Planetary Starcrafts closing in on them from a westerly intercept vector. Though still too far away to employ weapons, it wouldn't be long before they were under fire.

"Which is why they won't be guarding it. No one uses it. Once we exit the conduit, we will immediately take the next closest slipstream conduit. Hopefully our exposure to the Omegeon radiation will be brief."

"The slipstream map is incomplete in that region of space," Raviel reminded. "What if there isn't one close enough? What if we run out of time?"

Daeson glanced at the advancing Starcrafts.

"We don't have a choice. It's our one and only chance. The Omega Conduit terminates near the Haleo System, and I'm hoping we can find another exit conduit from there." Daeson realized that the Haleo System, the distant binary sister star to what had once been the Omega System, was dangerously close to the Omega Nebula, but he had no other idea.

"I hope you're right," she replied. "But you'd better adjust your course. The Agulla Asteroid Belt is dead ahead."

"I know." Daeson made a few more system adjustments as they transitioned from atmospheric flight to space flight. He directed his targeting computer to lock onto the leading two Starcrafts.

"You know?"

Daeson didn't like explaining everything he was doing when he needed to be concentrating.

"We have to go through it. It's massive, so we would never make it around with twelve Starcrafts on our tail. They're faster than us. Our only protection is in the belt itself."

Her silence told him she was worried. And she had every right to be. The odds of successfully navigating through an asteroid belt were extremely slim.

"See what you can do about increasing the power to our E-shield. We're going to need all the protection we can get."

"Roger that," came Raviel's confident reply.

She's tough, Daeson thought, reminding himself just how resourceful she also was. Having her skills in the back seat could prove to be invaluable. He marveled at her ability to think straight during dicey situations. Grabbing a flight processor interface module before launching had been a stroke of genius. She would be able to modify and adapt the Starcraft on the fly...an advantage no other pilot had.

Daeson would reach the edge of the Agulla Asteroid Belt just seconds before the other Starcrafts. He continued to accelerate until the last possible moment, hoping to increase their margin by a few more seconds. As they approached the field, the enormous size was daunting, and Daeson began to have second thoughts. He had practiced navigating the asteroid belt in the sim a few times just for kicks, but never had he tried to fly completely through it.

He decelerated to a speed at which he felt he could maneuver adequately. He was forced to alter his course multiple times to thwart any long range weapon attempts of the other Starcrafts. Now just seconds away from the belt, he could see that the asteroids ranged in size from small pebbles to several times larger than a Starcraft. Just as they were about to enter, the leading edge of the asteroid belt erupted in explosions. All twelve Starcrafts had unleashed a barrage of plasma bursts, hoping one would hit its mark before they entered the belt. As the plasma bursts missed and impacted the outer edge of the asteroids, the resulting fragmentation was extremely disorienting. Daeson hesitated, not sure of the path he had originally plotted. He altered his course once more and punched it.

Daeson focused exclusively on piloting the Starcraft at the maximum speed possible while still navigating between the larger asteroids. The sim hadn't done the actual asteroid field justice. This was unlike anything he had ever practiced before. It was a moment-by-moment series of life and death decisions.

"How large of an asteroid can the E-shield take?" he asked.

"Depends on closing velocity," Raviel replied, her voice tense but not panicked. "From what I'm seeing, melon-sized and below."

"That's not very comforting," Daeson said as he rolled, twisted, and turned in constant erratic maneuvering.

Thump! A fist-sized asteroid hit the leading edge of his right wing, causing an orange streak as the E-field deflected and pulverized it. A melon-sized rock grazed the top of the canopy.

"Whew!" Daeson exclaimed.

An asteroid to their left exploded into a thousand shards from a plasma burst.

"Great...they've entered and are behind us."

Daeson accelerated ever so slightly, pushing the limit of his piloting skills. He made for a large asteroid, inverted, and pulled around it to the opposite side, putting it between themselves and the pursuing Starcrafts. As he exited on the opposite side, he realized he was boxed in by three spinning asteroids, each the size of his Starcraft. When he opened fire on the nearest one, it split, allowing him to rotate his craft and dash between the two halves. Just clearing the opening, disaster waited on the other side. With no more space to maneuver, a boulder-sized asteroid outside of their plasma cannon's firing angle was on target to crush them. Daeson braced for impact, but at the last second, the asteroid's trajectory changed— almost as if it had been pushed away from them.

"What?" Daeson exclaimed.

"You're welcome," Raviel said enthusiastically.

"That was you?" Daeson asked, refocusing on the next few seconds of navigation. "How?"

"I reversed the polarity on the grappling field and turned it into a repulsion field. It should help us with some of the medium-sized asteroids. I just need a second or two to make the lock."

"That's amazing, Rav—!" He paused to juke left. "Well done!" he finished.

The plasma bursts continued at irregular intervals, but once Daeson and Raviel found a rhythm, he outdistanced the squadron. Before long it was evident that the squadron had either been destroyed or had abandoned their attempt to pursue. Daeson slowed the Starcraft to a more comfortable speed and focused on delivering them safely out of the field. After more than an hour of sheer consuming piloting, they exited the asteroid belt.

Daeson was exhausted. He tapped the coordinates to the Omega slipstream conduit entrance into the nav computer.

"That was incredible flying, Daeson. I never thought..."

"Take the stick, Rav."

"Really?"

"Yes, please take the stick...I need a moment."

He felt control of the Starcraft transfer to her and tilted his head back against the head rest. Every muscle in his body ached. Lifting his visor, he rubbed his eyes. He took a couple of deep breaths to help him relax his taut muscles.

"Daeson...we've got a problem!" Raviel's voice was thick with angst.

He opened his eyes and saw it first on his screen.

"Is that a..." Raviel began.

"A Jyptonian destroyer? Yes!"

"But how did it get here? I thought you said they wouldn't be guarding the Omega conduit entrance!"

"I have the Starcraft," Daeson said, shaking the stick to indicate he was back in control. How the destroyer got here didn't matter now...it was here. Four more Starcrafts appeared on the screen, having just launched from the destroyer.

Daeson plotted both their course to the Omega slipstream conduit entrance and the intercept course of the destroyer. Although he would arrive first, the weapons range of the plasma cannons on the destroyer were much greater, and Daeson knew his craft would never survive. There seemed little hope. The four Starcrafts were approaching rapidly and would be in weapons range within seconds.

"I'm sorry, Raviel. We don't have a chance against that destroyer. Once it's in range, one shot from its plasma cannon, and we're done."

"Then all we have to do is keep it from firing," Raviel said.

"I'm pretty sure that's not an option unless you can talk them out of it." Daeson's frustration was evident in his tone.

"They're not going to fire on their own Starcraft, are they?" Raviel asked.

"You're a genius!" Daeson exclaimed.

Daeson immediately banked the Starcraft and took up a flight path that positioned the flight of the four Starcrafts directly between him and the destroyer. It was not a direct route to the conduit entrance, but it would buy them time and distance. The maneuver was smart, but it only prolonged the inevitable. The E-shield could take two or perhaps three hits from the other Starcrafts before suffering major damage.

Daeson accelerated to full speed, but it still would not be enough. The Planetary Aero Force A32 Starcrafts had newer more powerful engines that would give them a 20% speed advantage over Daeson and Raviel's Starcraft. In addition, once they were in range, he would have to fly a random zigzag pattern to thwart any long-range cannon bursts. He incrementally adjusted his flight path toward the conduit. At some point he would have to abandon the cat and mouse game and make a run for it, but not yet.

"They're firing!" Raviel warned.

A moment later two bursts screamed passed, narrowly missing their right wing and engine.

"I don't want to leave this to chance. Can we project the line of fire so I can react?"

"Yes, but you'd have less than 1.6 seconds to respond, and the time would diminish as they closed in on us," Raviel replied.

"That's all I need."

A few seconds later the display before him changed to show a target with concentric rings around a rear view of their Starcraft.

"Incoming!" Raviel exclaimed.

The display showed a cannon burst growing in the upper right quadrant. Daeson dived low and left just as the burst whizzed past. Soon the display filled with three more bursts. Daeson could gauge the position and range by the display Raviel put before him.

"This works, Rav...nice job!"

He mustered the mental energy necessary to once more pilot in a way he had never prepared for. Maneuvering left, right, up, and down, he was able to thwart each burst, but his time to react was diminishing quickly.

Wham! A plasma burst slammed into his left wing near the engine nacelle. The E-shield strength immediately dropped to 74%.

"They're too close. I can't react fast enough!"

"We're still sixty seconds from the conduit entrance," Raviel replied. "And that destroyer is getting awfully close too. What's the range of its cannons?"

Daeson saw two of the pursuing Starcrafts peel off to the left, while the other two went right.

"I'd say about here," Daeson said.

He gave up on using the Starcrafts as protection and changed his flight path for a direct route straight to the conduit entrance. A fraction of a second later a massive plasma cannon burst ripped through the space they had just abandoned. Daeson's stomach went up to his throat. One hit would obliterate them.

He heard Raviel gasp. "What now?" Raviel's voice no longer hid the panic swelling up within her.

Daeson quickly ran through his options, but there were none. No way out. They were still twenty-five seconds from the entrance.

"Sovereign Ell Yon, please help us if you can," Raviel whispered the words.

Daeson shook his head. *Meaningless superstition!* he thought.

Daeson pulled up just as another massive cannon burst passed beneath them. He rolled and realigned back on course to the conduit entrance. Fifteen seconds. He flipped up the guard covering his slipstream jump drive switch.

"Come on...just a few more seconds!" Daeson voiced unconsciously.

"Incoming!" Raviel shouted.

There was no time to react. Just seconds from escape, they would be utterly destroyed. The remaining fraction of a second slowed, and Daeson's last thought before the final hit was deep sorrow for Raviel. She didn't deserve this—he had killed her. He was the reason the galaxy would exist without her beautiful soul.

The brilliant white hot plasma was on them, but at the last moment it blasted into something just off his right wing. The impact illumined the shape of a cloaked galactic warship he had never seen before. Chills flowed up and down his body as the brief but distinct outline of something far beyond their technology absorbed the energy of the destroyer's weapon and then quickly disappeared. In a near stupor at what had just happened, Daeson nearly forgot the conduit entrance.

He engaged the jump drive, and the space around them melted. In an instant the Starcrafts, the destroyer, and whatever that cloaked figment was had disappeared. The conduit walls gave glimpses of white streaks as stars came and went. This would be the longest slipstream jump Daeson had ever made, and the visual effects inside were stunning. The walls of the conduit were transparent wisps of a protective sheath that was surely alien in design.

After a few seconds, Raviel whispered, "It's beautiful."

"What just happened back there?" Daeson asked, still confounded by their escape.

"I don't know. What do you think it was?"

Daeson quickly looked over the slipstream jump drive parameters—all normal.

"Something massive," Daeson replied. "Some advanced technology ship from another planet. Jypton sure doesn't have anything like that."

"From everything I've read, cloaking technology that perfect isn't possible. And the shape was...well whatever that thing was, it wasn't manmade."

Daeson huffed. "What are you suggesting, Raviel?"

After a long pause, Daeson heard Raviel click the com button.

"There's only one answer. It was one of Sovereign Ell Yon's...a ship of the Immortals."

Daeson shook his head. "There are no Immortals! That superstitious legend is for children's stories."

"I see. Well that superstitious legend just saved your hide!"

"Uh-huh. How about you focus on scanning for slipstream conduits. The closer we get to the nebula, the more accurate our scans should be. Once we hit radiated space, we're going to need an exit soon."

Before he had finished his words, the slipstream map appeared on his display, showing conduits as the scanner picked them up. The smile on his face faded. The closest conduit was highlighted, with its distance flashing red. He waited until they were within sixty seconds of exiting and the scans were complete before acknowledging.

"Is this accurate?" he asked.

"There is some interference I can't account for, but as far as our scanner can detect, I'm afraid so."

The Omega Nebula slipstream conduit exit was seconds away. Behind them was a Jyptonian destroyer and its fleet of Starcrafts. Before them was a section of space near the Omega Nebula that was uninhabitable because of the deadly Omegeon radiation. They were out of time and out of options.

CHAPTER

11

Curse of the Nebula

"I'm sorry, Rav," Daeson lamented as the Starcraft's slipstream engine automatically disengaged at the exit of the conduit. "Looks like I flew us into a corner."

The walls of the conduit disintegrated like stardust in an atmosphere, and the melted fabric of space reformed around them. Before them was the Haleo System and its twelve planets, but it was eclipsed in splendor by the Omega Nebula, just 0.3 light years away. Even at this distance, the size of the nebula was staggering. Their canopy was filled with an epic display of brilliant colors shrouded in dense plasma clouds that flashed in constant bursts of frighteningly beautiful energy. Daeson could almost make himself believe it was a living creature that would reach out and swallow them in an instant. It was majestic!

"Breathtaking," Raviel breathed.

"Ironic that something this beautiful is so deadly," Daeson stated flatly. "This is more than a supernova remnant nebula. Look how dense it is—almost like it's a barrier."

"From preliminary measurements, it isn't expanding or contracting," Raviel chimed in.

Daeson lingered a few seconds in awestruck wonder before engaging his engines. He noticed that Raviel displayed the Omegeon radiation level on his display.

"How long do you think we have?" she asked.

"Not sure...not long enough to get away or make it to the next conduit. That's for sure." Daeson couldn't hide his discouragement. "The Haleo System has one planet that has a breathable atmosphere, but it puts us even closer to the nebula."

"The sixth planet, Mesos," Raviel's voice carried a sense of awe.

Daeson punched in the coordinates for the planet Mesos, once the home world of one of the most advanced civilizations the galaxy had ever known, the very cradle of humanity. The display seemed blurry. "If we can make it to the planet, there's a chance we might find something that will shield us from the Omegeon radiation."

"Not likely," Raviel rebutted. "Omegeon radiation penetrates just about everything."

Daeson didn't reply.

"Will we make it?" she asked. "Maybe it's in my head, but I'm already not feeling well, Daeson." Her voice quavered.

Daeson blinked hard to clear his vision. The Omegeon radiation couldn't be affecting him this quickly could it?

"We'll make it," he said as confidently as he could muster.

"Why aren't there any other slipstream conduits?" Raviel asked.

"When the Omega Star went supernova," Daeson had to concentrate to finish, "it must have collapsed all of the other...conduits. It looks like the one we just came through...is the only remaining conduit here."

"Are you okay?"

"Yeah...I'm good," he lied.

Daeson accelerated the Starcraft toward Mesos, adjusting slightly for Galeo, the large moon in orbit around the planet. He held the velocity until the last possible moment—the planet loomed large before them. Within a few minutes, he was transitioning to atmospheric flight in what had to be a record reentry time. His arms and legs began to ache. He had to will them to move; no longer were his actions natural. It now took every bit of energy left in him to focus and fly the ship.

Raviel seemed to understand and stayed as quiet as possible. She scanned the planet and typed in landing coordinates near an abandoned city that was close to their reentry point. Time was running out, and in the haze of his reasoning, Daeson questioned his intent. Perhaps dying in a fiery Starcraft impact would be preferable to a drawn-out death by Omegeon poisoning.

"Rav...how are...you doing?" he asked as he extended the landing struts. Just the final descent to go now.

"I'm feeling it, Daeson, but I'm okay. Are you?"

Every muscle now resisted. His aches were replaced with pain. Daeson shook his head to clear the fog and then blinked hard so he could see the readings on the display. He struggled to remember the proper landing numbers. Clearly, it was too late for him, but perhaps Raviel would still have a chance. Oh, how futile their efforts had been!

"This could be a rough...landing. Hang on," he warned.

The Starcraft wobbled as Daeson fought for control. Just a few more feet. He felt one of the struts touch and then slammed the throttles back to cut power to the engines. The Starcraft lurched downward on the left side, and he heard the struts bottom out...but the Starcraft had landed.

"I'm sorry, Rav...I...I..." Daeson couldn't remember what he was going to say. Pain came in waves.

"Aahhh!" he screamed and doubled over. He was barely cognizant of Raviel's pulling him out of the cockpit and forcing him to climb down the ladder with her.

He tried to push her away to get her to save herself, but he had no strength to resist. She laid him on the ground beneath the Starcraft.

The excruciating pain erased the mental fog he had earlier experienced. Now his skin felt like it was being burned from his body. He opened his eyes and looked up at Raviel. Her eyes were wide with fear. No—horror. Tears swelled in her eyes. She reached out and touched his cheek with her hand. Why did she still look so beautiful?

Another avalanche of pain hit Daeson until his mind emptied itself of every thought. Then the world went black.

Daeson opened his eyes to an existence laced with nausea and pain. He had never been so miserable in all his life. His whole body felt numb and immovable, as if he were encased in hardened resin. Why wasn't he dead? A presence waited beside him, but he knew not who. He slowly forced his head to turn to his right. There beside him lay Raviel. Her lovely face was ashen as though dead. *I've killed her.* Tears fell from his eyes and trickled down his cheek.

This lonely death on a poisoned planet was not what Raviel deserved. He now realized that her hand was in his, so he squeezed. Her eyes opened, and his heart jumped. She slowly turned her head toward him until their eyes met. Nothing was said, but in that final moment of life, he loved her. If only he could speak the words. But he saw love in her eyes too, and it was enough. He closed his eyes, knowing Raviel would be the last vision he would behold.

Daeson felt the coolness in his mouth but didn't know what to do with it. Something wet trickled down his chin from the corner of his mouth and onto his neck. Swallow—it was hard to remember how. He could feel the chilled water go down his throat and into his stomach; it was the first pleasant sensation he'd had since...since his death. How long ago had that been? Hours...days...weeks? The notes of a distant song lingered in his mind as he forced his way to full consciousness. He opened his eyes, but they resisted him. The figure above him cleared, and the smile on Raviel's face was better than the water he'd swallowed. In spite of her smile, tears were in her eyes, but he didn't know why. He felt her hand touch his face.

"You're still alive," she whispered. A tear fell onto his cheek. It was a warm contrast to the coolness of the water. "I thought I'd lost you."

Daeson tried to talk, but he could make no sounds. Raviel trickled a little more water into his mouth. He swallowed it easier this time.

"How...how long?" his raspy whisper came.

Raviel's eyebrows furrowed. "It's been two weeks."

Two weeks! *How am I...how are we still alive?* he wondered.

When Daeson lifted his hand, it felt weighted down by nine g's of gravity. As Raviel put her hand in his, he saw what had happened...what he had become. His hand and arm were mere bones with gray-colored flesh hanging from them. He was a ghost of a man. His eyes widened in alarm as he looked back to Raviel. She pushed his hand down and came close to his face.

"You're alive, Daeson...that's what matters right now!"

Chills of fright went up and down his entire body. He tried to sit up, but there was no strength left in him. The Omegeon particles had ravaged him completely. What a cruel way to die: weeks of deterioration, a slow and agonizing withering away to nothing. He looked at Raviel and realized something was different about her. Not only had she survived, but she nearly glowed.

"What is happening?" Daeson croaked. "You...you look—" He held up his hand to her cheek, and she leaned into his hand.

Her skin was full of color, not death like his. Her eyes were full of life.

"I don't know, Daeson, but you're going to live. Today is the first day of a new life for you. Somehow I just know it. Hang on!" His arm fell to his side, and he lost consciousness once again.

Over the next few days, Raviel nursed Daeson back to life. He could do little more than eat and drink before falling back asleep. She had found a nearby stream to draw fresh water from. The rations from the Starcraft had run out five days ago, so she had ventured into the forest and discovered edible berries and roots as food. She had also made a makeshift tent over the nose of the Starcraft as a shelter.

Daeson finally felt well enough to sit up, and it took every ounce of energy he had to accomplish it, even with Raviel's help. He leaned against the leading strut of the Starcraft, taking a minute for the dizziness in his brain to dispel.

"How long were you out?" Daeson asked. It was the first time since landing on Mesos that he felt he had a coherent thought.

"According to the Starcraft clock, I was out two days."

"Why isn't the Omegeon radiation affecting you like it is me? And why am I not dead?"

Raviel encouraged him to drink from the flask, but he wanted answers more than food and water.

She sat down next to him.

"I'm not completely sure—we should both be dead. As for our differences right now, I think it has to do with the levels of Deitum Prime in our bodies."

Daeson frowned. "What do you mean? Why would that have anything to do with it?"

"The Omegeon radiation...I think its purging Deitum Prime from our bodies." She looked over at Daeson, her eyes aglow. "At first I was affected like you—nauseated and so sick I wanted to die. But it quickly went away. Now..." Raviel looked at her hand as she slowly closed her fingers to form a fist. "Now I feel amazing...like new life has been injected into my veins."

Daeson held up his arm, still finding it difficult to believe it belonged to him. Frail, gray, and weak. "That's not how I feel," he moaned. "I think I should die at any moment. I have no muscle, my skin is gray like death, and I am weak to the point of passing out from the exertion of breathing."

He turned and looked at Raviel. She did look amazing.

"If what you are saying is true, it's almost as if I have to die first to be alive."

Raviel nodded. "Yes, I suppose that is true."

Daeson thought for a moment and then shook his head. "Your theory doesn't make sense."

"It does if you consider how much more Deitum Prime you had in your body than I did. It has been the purpose of my people to abstain from anything tainted with Deitum Prime for centuries. And although that has been impossible, considering how it has been infused into almost all water and food supplies, we have ways to limit it."

Daeson considered Raviel's words. "It still doesn't make sense. Radiation in any form is always harmful."

"It's true that radiation causes biological changes in our cells, but when that radiation is designed to destroy alien genetic mutations, I would call that helpful not harmful. The galaxy believes that Omegeon radiation poisons, but we, as Rayleans, know that the truth is quite different. Omeganite and its radiation is a powerful source of energy with profound characteristics that we are only just beginning to understand. Omeganite crystals have remarkable properties."

Daeson shook his head. "The way you think and the things you believe are so strange. You do realize that it's you against the galaxy? That your theories are conspiracies of galactic proportion?"

Raviel turned to face him more directly. "It *is* a conspiracy, Daeson. The galaxy has been deceived by the Scourge! We may seem like the insignificant Drudge to the Jyptonians and a dozen other worlds, but Sovereign Ell Yon sees us as something quite different." Raviel looked past Daeson and into the future. "One day an Immortal will become mortal and live among us. He will change everything. The oracles call him 'the Merchant'."

Daeson's eyes furrowed. "Why Merchant?"

"Because one day he will purchase us and set us free from the prison of Deitum Prime."

"And bring about the Reclamation," Daeson finished. He knew his tone was heavy with condescension, but he was too discouraged to care. Daeson's gaze fell to his legs, once strong and powerful, but now too weak to even carry his own weight. "I must look appalling to you," he said, turning away from her.

Raviel lifted her hand to his chin and forced him to look back at her. "You look beautiful to me, Daeson, because you're alive."

Daeson pushed her hand away. "I want to see myself."

Raviel frowned. "Not yet."

Daeson glared at her. "I want to see!"

Raviel hesitated before climbing up to the cockpit and returning with her glass tablet. She handed it to him.

He looked into the glass and just stared at the creature staring back—a wisp of a man, gaunt, gray, and hollow. The talented and handsome Daeson

Lockridge of Jypton was gone. He touched his cheek bone where the fabric of some death-colored skin hung. "So this is the real me...the me without Deitum Prime?"

Raviel said nothing. After a few more seconds of Daeson's gazing at the horror before him, Raviel put a gentle hand on his and pushed the glass away. She got on her knees and held his face in her hands. "This isn't the end of you, Daeson...it's the beginning."

Daeson tried to look away, but she wouldn't let him. "I'm here for you...we're going to get you through this."

Finally he looked deep into her eyes. "I felt betrayed when I discovered who you really were."

Raviel leaned back and her gaze went to the ground.

"But on that day...the day Linden arrested you in the hangar...you stopped me from defending you...from incriminating myself," Daeson said, mesmerized by each curve of her face. "It was that act which made me believe there was something real between us...that perhaps I was more than just an intelligence target...more than a mere mark."

She looked back up to him.

"You sacrificed yourself...innocent, perfect, and beautiful," Daeson said, remembering the Crimson Rose ritual she had shared with him on the beach weeks ago.

Raviel shook her head. "I am none of those," she said.

"You are to me," he replied. It was his turn to look away, remembering the image he had just seen of himself. She reached out and touched his arm, but he wanted to pull away. He couldn't imagine why she wasn't repulsed by him. He needed to shift their conversation, so he thought about Raviel's theory regarding Deitum Prime. Much of it made sense, but it seemed so preposterous that he could hardly bring himself to accept it. He cleared his throat.

"How can you tell how much Deitum Prime has been assimilated by the body?" he asked.

She leaned back off her knees and sat down next to him once more. "We can't, really. Every person is different. We haven't been able to develop a method to comprehensively test the human body or any living organism for that matter. That's partly why it's so difficult to abstain from it."

Daeson sat in silent contemplation for a long while, and Raviel didn't disturb him. She busied herself with improving their shelter and foraging for more food. In spite of the extreme and deplorable condition of his body, there was a stillness in his soul that he had never experienced before. *Why?* He wondered.

The next few days brought marginal improvement in Daeson's condition. He hated being nursed. It made him feel so weak...so vulnerable. But that is exactly what he was—and worse. He held up his arm and gazed at the thin, gaunt appendage. He could hardly stand and then for just a moment or two.

Raviel, on the other hand, seemed to be operating at an entirely new level of energy and endurance. His recovery, if it could even be called such, was slow and discouraging. Conversing with Raviel kept Daeson going. He slowly began to understand the deeper things of who she was and why she believed the way she did. And with each discovery, he was all the more fascinated with her.

With the day nearly spent, the moon Galeo began to shine its full splendor in the night sky, their view only slightly obstructed by the nose of their Starcraft. On the horizon, the moon looked even larger than it should have, filling much of the lower western sky. A few of the brighter stars began to shine in the ebbing day.

"It's beautiful," Raviel said. "Like you said, out among the stars it is both frightful and amazing."

Daeson gazed at the brightening blue and white globe. "There's something about it."

Raviel looked over at him. "What do you mean?"

Daeson shook his head. "I'm not sure. Something about Galeo is...unusual. It's large enough to have an atmosphere. Legends say it was colonized by the people of Mesos, but no one has ventured here for thousands of years to verify it. Can't help but wonder."

"It is remarkable...peaceful," Raviel added.

Something deep inside Daeson was aching...for something he knew not, but gazing at Galeo intensified the inexplicable feeling. He looked over at Raviel.

"When I came to, a song lingered in my head."

Raviel glanced at him before turning her gaze back to Galeo.

"That was you, wasn't it?"

She fidgeted.

"What is the song?" Daeson asked.

Ravel dropped her gaze to her hands. "It's a lullaby my mother used to sing to me when I was a child."

"Will you sing it for me now?"

Raviel's cheeks flushed. "I don't think so. I'm not a singer like my mother. Her voice is—"

"Please?" Daeson petitioned.

Raviel looked over at him and then to the stars. A moment later her voice lifted in beautiful, soothing notes that stirred Daeson's heart. Words of hope and promise that he didn't understand enticed his soul in the strangest of ways.

"In Misty Stars beyond there lies
The dreams of bright and youthful eyes.
A place where hope in all comes true
That's wise and free and good and new.

There's one that seeks a heart that's pure,
Whose strength and confidence is sure
For with that soul are battles won
Immortals hands not be undone.

He comes to set the captives free,
And win the hearts of you and me.
For from the stars his grace shall fall
On meek and lowly, poor and small.

So dream your dreams and lift your eyes
From hill and vale to lofty skies,
And fly beyond the stars of old
And walk the paths of legends bold.

At journey's end he'll favor few
Just those whose hearts for him were true.
Midst stars and nebula he'll crown
The noble, loyal glory bound!

In the Nova shone his light
A guide to wintry eons' night.
His name you'll wear upon your chest
From sword and battle then you'll rest."

Her final note slipped away into the evening sky and left Daeson mesmerized.

"That was absolutely beautiful," Daeson said, unable to turn his gaze away from her. "It reminds me of the music of our dance...hopeful yet strangely forlorn."

Raviel looked back to Daeson. "It is the hope of our people...the promise of Ell Yon."

Daeson was undeniably moved by the song. Something about it felt like so much more than a child's lullaby. It was so…real.

Raviel stood up. "I'd best find us some food and water before nightfall sets in."

Daeson grabbed her hand. "Be careful. Okay?"

Raviel squeezed his hand. "Of course. But I haven't come across anything so far that is even remotely dangerous. This planet is unusual to say the least."

Raviel left camp, her lilting words hanging in Daeson's thoughts. His lack of strength and ability to protect her was frustrating. He wondered how long they could keep this up. Was he really growing stronger, or was death an eventuality? He worked up the energy to gather some kindling and a few pieces of wood to start a fire. Setting his Talon on its lowest setting, he ignited the kindling and soon had a fire that glowed in the alien dusk of Mesos. Daeson wondered at the comfort that something as simple as a fire could bring. He realized that such comfort is only found at the emptying of all amenities, and until now, that had never been his experience.

Fatigue was setting in again. As he was moving to lie down, the hairs on the back of Daeson's neck stood straight. Someone or something was near. He grabbed his Talon, charged it, and extended the blade. Though the shadows of the day were long, there was still enough light to see quite well, and yet…

Daeson stood and circled their camp, trying to portray what little strength he had. "Raviel?"

Nothing.

He tried to quell his jitters, but they soon turned to fear. He circled around again—nothing.

"Get a hold of yourself, Lockridge. There's nothing here."

"Daeson!" A deep, rich voice nearly shook him from the inside out. He jerked about as quickly as he could, leading with his Talon. There before him stood a hooded man, his arms crossed.

"Keep clear...I'm armed," Daeson warned. The adrenaline was carrying the moment, but he was quickly losing his strength.

The man stared back at him. There was something frightening yet peaceful about him. When he walked toward Daeson, Daeson readied his Talon, but when the man was just two paces away, the Talon's blade retracted, and the charged plasma chamber powered down. Daeson glanced down at the useless weapon and tried to power it back up, but it wouldn't respond. He lifted his eyes to the man who stood before him and tried to absorb the steel-eyed gaze of absolute power. The man slowly lifted the hood from his head and let the fabric fall to his majestic shoulders. Daeson immediately felt small...insignificant. Chills ran up and down his spine until he trembled. Was this fear?

The man's head tilted ever so slightly. His eyes nearly burned with the flames of Immortal power.

"You are here for a reason, Daeson Starlore. I've chosen you."

"How do you know that name?" Daeson asked.

"You've lived a privileged life. It takes time for one such as you to begin to see the truth." The man watched Daeson as if evaluating him.

"What truth?"

"That there is much more than what you see."

"Who are you?" he whispered.

"Who do you think I am?" the man said. Daeson couldn't withdraw from those eyes—deep, compassionate, powerful, Immortal. Somehow he knew who this was. The Rayleans revered him; the

Torians feared him. The galaxy thought him a myth, but here he was, standing before Daeson.

"You are the hope the Rayleans cling to in their bondage."

"I am."

"You are the Immortal of the Raylean legends."

"I am."

"You are...the Sovereign Ell Yon."

"I am!"

Could this be true? Daeson wondered. A wave of nausea overwhelmed him. His strength was nearly depleted. Surely this was another hallucinative effect of the Omegeon radiation. Daeson faltered, almost collapsing to the ground, but Ell Yon reached for him. Strength and life seemed to flow through his warm touch, and Daeson recovered.

"What is happening to me?" Daeson asked, holding up his hand. "Why hasn't the Omegeon radiation killed me?"

"You are being purged," Ell Yon answered.

Daeson shook his head as Raviel's words rang in his mind.

"Purged...from Deitum Prime?"

"Yes. Omeganite's radiation isn't poisonous; it is life and power. It destroys any Deitum Prime it comes in contact with and restores the essence of all that should be. This place," Ell Yon motioned to the world around him, "is a place nearly pure from Deitum Prime."

"But I'm wasting away to nothing," Daeson said, looking down at his frail arm.

"This," Sovereign Ell Yon glanced down at Daeson's arm, "is who you have always been. What you were was an illusion of Deitum Prime. But don't despair. One day you will be a strong leader of the Rayleans, a warrior of the Navi!"

Daeson was once again confused by his words. *What did this mean?*

"I don't understand. The Rayleans have been and always will be the servants of Jypton."

"If that is what you believe, then you do not yet know me. When you're stronger, I will call you."

Sovereign Ell Yon looked once more into Daeson's eyes, revealing a regal power in his gaze that caused Daeson to shudder. Then he turned and walked away. The image of the man shifted and bent until he was gone.

"Daeson...Daeson!"

Raviel was shaking his shoulder. When Daeson opened his eyes, she looked worried.

"What...what is it?"

"I thought you were...here sit up."

Daeson realized that he had crumpled in a heap next to the fire. His legs were sore and cramped from the awkward position.

"Are you okay?" she asked, helping him to a sitting position.

The fire was smoldering—its fuel expired.

"Yes, I think so."

"What happened to you?" she asked. She wouldn't let go of him.

The conversation with the hooded man came back to him. *Was it all a dream? The hallucination seemed so real.*

"I'm not sure. I thought I saw some...thing." He looked at her. Her countenance filled with worry, her strength shattered in a moment.

"Don't do that to me again."

He reached up and put an arm around her, and she sank into him.

"Don't ever do that to me again," she whispered.

CHAPTER

12

An Ancient Foe

And one will rise in the midst of you, and he will lead you in the way of the Navi. – Sabella, Oracle of Ell Yon

Day by day Daeson regained his strength. With each miniscule improvement, Raviel seemed overjoyed and oddly more distant. He wondered at her strength...her determination. On the day he was finally able to hike with her for an hour without collapsing, he stopped her on the top of a knoll overlooking the nearby ancient Mesosian city. He was breathing hard, but he felt good. They gazed at the marvel of the cityscape and imagined it in all its former glory.

"Thanks, Raviel...for not giving up on me."

She put her hands on her hips and took a deep breath.

"I didn't have much of a choice. I don't know how to fly that Starcraft...wouldn't want to be stranded here all by myself." She looked at him and smiled.

"Oh, I see," Daeson smirked.

She shoved him, and he laughed.

"So what are you up for?" Raviel asked.

"Well, I'm still only half the man I once was...or rather should be. I still have a long way to go, but in the meantime, we should explore that city," he responded, looking out toward the mysterious relic.

Raviel smiled wide. "Let's go!"

They descended the knoll and walked along what must have once been a transportation rail.

Raviel seemed deep in thought.

"What's on your mind?" Daeson asked.

She glanced over at him. "Have you thought much about home?"

Daeson had to admit that he had thought about not only his mother, but also Tig and Raviel's family. He nodded.

"I'm sick with worry over my parents...all of Drudgetown for that matter," Raviel acknowledged.

"I know. I am too. I try not to think about it because there's nothing we can do."

But it was impossible not to think about, and there was no way of knowing. Communication at this distance was out of the question. It would take decades for any radio transmissions to reach them.

"I shudder to think about what might be happening to our people. I think you've been kept in the dark about just how ruthless the Chancellor and his Elite can be when it comes to us Rayleans," Raviel said with an edge of anger in her voice.

Daeson looked over at Raviel and caught her eye. "I'm beginning to realize," Daeson said, shaking his head as he thought of his mother's story and then of Tig's. He imagined that these stories were more common than not. "I had no idea. I hate that I was so ignorant to the maltreatment of your people...our people."

"We have to go back, Daeson. I can hardly stand not knowing...not being there to help them."

Daeson stopped walking and grabbed Raviel's arm. "Look, I feel it too, but right now I don't even have enough strength to fly that Starcraft, let alone face the Jyptonian Empire."

Raviel nodded. "Yes, but at some point we have to do something!"

Daeson couldn't help the crooked smile that crossed his lips. "I can see why the Plexus chose you."

Raviel didn't smile back. She looked away.

"They didn't choose me...I chose them."

They resumed their journey into the city but at a much slower pace. Daeson matched her gait. Her instantly somber mood sobered him.

"How so?" he gently asked.

Raviel looked over at him, hesitation in her eyes. Whatever the story, pain was there.

"When someone you love is murdered...it changes you," Raviel said.

Daeson had nothing with which to respond. He just waited. Slowly Raviel began to tell him the tragic story of her sister Aliza. When she was through, they walked in silence for a time. It helped Daeson to understand her better, but it did more than that. His eyes were slowly being opened to the truth about the Lockridge family—about the darkness there. It sickened him knowing that he had been an ignorant part of it for so long.

"I'm truly sorry."

Raviel nodded, but her steely-eyed countenance lingered. How could she not still blame him for at least some of her lingering pain?

They ventured into the city and explored a few of the buildings near its perimeter. Something was eerie about such colossal emptiness. The technology they observed was impressive for a civilization that had existed over a millennium ago. In many ways, it seemed to exceed even their own. Each day they journeyed further into the city, fascinated by what they discovered. One building in particular was filled with technological wonders. Daeson could hardly get Raviel to leave. She was nearly giddy with excitement as she explored and collected various pieces of ancient tech.

"We need to get back to the Starcraft, Rav," Daeson urged, but Raviel was completely mesmerized by a device smaller than her hand.

She looked up at Daeson, eyes open wide.

"I think these people were beginning to utilize Omeganite in their tech."

"Why is that so important?" Daeson asked. "What advantage does Omeganite have with technology?"

Raviel walked over to Daeson to show him the device. "Our ancient oracles were given the knowledge of technology capable of utilizing one of the amazing properties of Omeganite."

"Omeganite does more than just emit Omegeon particles?"

Raviel nodded. "Much more. The problem is that the Omegeon particles are so deadly and the shielding required so elaborate that we have only scratched the surface. In its natural form, Omeganite is crystalline. An Omeganite crystal the size of a grain of sand emits enough Omegeon particles to kill a small city. Of course the higher the concentration of Deitum Prime, the deadlier the exposure. That's why every other race in the galaxy won't touch it," Raviel explained.

"I get that," Daeson said. "I still can't believe I'm alive. So what property do the oracles use?"

Raviel smiled. "Communication."

Daeson tilted his head. "How?"

"Omeganite crystals emit Omegeon particles and photons that allow instantaneous communication via the quantum entanglement principle."

Daeson smirked. "That's impossible. You're telling me that back on Jypton, Rayleans are using Omeganite crystals to communicate instantaneously across the globe."

"How do you think the Plexus has remained undetected for the last one hundred years?"

"But I thought the quantum entanglement principle was just a theory," Daeson replied.

Raviel shook her head. "Not just a theory. We discovered that no matter the distance—ten feet or ten quintillion light years—entangled Omeganite crystals can be used to transmit and receive data instantaneously and completely undetected since there is no electromagnetic transmission to intercept."

Daeson ran his fingers through his hair. "That is more than remarkable. I had no idea."

He turned his gaze back to the device in Raviel's hand. "Is that an Omeganite communicator?"

"It's much smaller than mine, but yes, I believe so."

Daeson's eyes opened wide.

"Yours? You're telling me only now that you have a way to communicate with Jypton? Seriously?"

"It's one of the reasons I had to go back and get my pack before we left Jypton. If that were to fall into Jyptonian hands..." Raviel shook her head. "But it doesn't matter. The communicator has been dark since we left." She seemed lost in thought. Daeson knew she was thinking of home again.

"Why?" Daeson asked.

"The Plexus knew I had been captured, and they would have to assume that everything associated with me was compromised."

"But have you tried contacting them...explaining our situation?"

"Yes, a hundred times, but there is too much at risk. Imagine if there were Jyptonian agents that were posing as me. The entire Plexus would be exposed. No, I'm afraid my communicator is as worthless as this one."

Daeson's hope of word from home faded as quickly as it had come. They both fell silent.

Just then a loud crashing sound shattered the surrounding silence. Raviel nearly dropped the communicator, and Daeson instinctively reached for his Talon. They looked at each other, Daeson's heart racing.

"It came from above," Raviel said quietly.

"Probably just something that was ready to collapse—"

Loud scraping noises abruptly ended his explanation. Daeson charged his Talon as they made their way to a broad stairway that led up to the next level of the building. He looked at Raviel, and she nodded. They began carefully navigating each dusty step. The scraping noises grew louder as they ascended. The sound was too consistent...too man-made. Daeson weighed the risk, carefully considering his weakened state, but his curiosity wouldn't let him turn away. As they neared the top of the stairwell, the scraping sound stopped, and so did Daeson and Raviel. Had they been detected? They paused before moving onward. Crouching near the top pedestal, they scanned the large open room for some clue as to the noise.

"Look at the tech here," Raviel said. "It looks like an ancient robotics facility."

Daeson nodded. Work benches, shelves, and storage bins held mechanical arms, legs, and heads. Raviel and Daeson worked their way toward one of the benches, and Daeson picked up a dusty mechanical arm. Something inside him shivered as he recalled his history lessons.

"I don't like this," Daeson said. "Mesos was the origination point of the Artificial Intelligence Rebellion that led to the AI Wars."

Frightful tales were often told late at night about the ruthless methods of the bots during the AI wars. AI had been the culmination of humanity's intelligence. The advent of AI was supposed to bring humanity into a new existence, ushering in an era of peace, unity, and ease. But what the geniuses of AI failed to consider was that the easiest aspects of mankind to emulate were those that were the most destructive: the quest for knowledge, power, and control.

The resulting wars first ravaged Mesos, causing many to flee the planet, which propelled the spread of mankind to other regions of space. Using slipstream conduits, some people fled to the far reaches of the galaxy, desperately seeking to escape the horrors of ruthless and brutal robot attacks. But the AI bots followed. Humanity was in a desperate fight for its very survival.

For hundreds of years, the AI wars continued and spread throughout the galaxy until one man, Elias Boson, discovered the secret to defeating the machines and led the war against them. Sector by sector and planet by planet, the galaxy destroyed the AI bots until few remained. In a final attempt to retaliate and isolate the forces of humanity, the AI bots found a way to destroy many of the slipstream conduits that connected this region of the galaxy with the outer planets.

Humanity had been splintered, without any way of contacting or traveling to the farthest inhabited planets. Without the supply of trade ships and the abundant resources of the cradle of humanity, the chances that any had survived in the outer planets were slim. When the AI wars ended, strict anti-AI code rules were unilaterally agreed upon and enforced.

Daeson set the mechanical arm back on the table and looked at Raviel. "What if—"

"I beg your pardon. May I be of assistance?" A mellow voice shattered the silence of the room as an android rose up from a pile of rubble just behind them.

Daeson and Raviel jolted away as Daeson aimed his Talon at the machine standing just in front them, his finger partially depressing the discharge trigger. The adrenaline coursing through his legs was almost too much for him in his weakened state. The android looked at Daeson as if he were waiting for instruction.

"Magnificent!" Raviel said, staring at the technological wonder. A perfectly engineered assembly of mechanical wizardry stood eye to eye with her. He didn't have the synthetic skin overlay that had covered most of the AI robots of the past.

Raviel took a step toward it, but Daeson grabbed her arm. "What are you doing? This thing could be programmed to take your head off. It was obviously built before the galactic AI restriction codes were in place. Except for the absence of skin, it looks like a human, talks like a human, and walks like a human."

Raviel seemed nearly hypnotized by the machine but proceeded no further. Daeson leaned close to Raviel, not taking his eyes or the aim of his Talon off the machine.

"I should blast it right now," he whispered. "This thing is probably in violation of every one of the ten anti-AI restriction codes."

"We don't know that," Raviel countered.

"How may I be of assistance?" the android repeated in a warm and friendly voice.

Raviel shook her head. "It could have attacked and killed us before we knew it was here. I don't think it's programmed to kill."

Daeson considered Raviel's statement.

"What is your purpose?" he asked the android.

"I am a maintenance android. It is my duty to ensure this facility is properly cleaned and organized."

Daeson looked around at the disheveled room. "Doesn't look like you're doing a very good job."

"How may I be of assistance?" the android asked once more.

Daeson looked at Raviel, his eyebrow raised.

"Doesn't seem too bright either," he said. "How is it possible that it's still functioning after thousands of years?"

"There must be a charging station that is still working." Raviel couldn't help herself as she stepped forward again. "Look at the joint structures...its technology is remarkable."

Then without warning, the robot turned and began walking toward a table. One of its legs was malfunctioning, so the robot had to drag the leg behind. As it walked away, Daeson lowered his Talon. Raviel walked to catch up to it.

"Be careful, Raviel. Even if it's not AI, it could be dangerous."

"It's just a droid," she said. "Our world has thousands of them."

"Yes, but none of them look like that one."

"Android, stop," Raviel said. The android stopped and looked at her.

"How may I be of assistance?" the android said.

"What is your designation?"

"I am RI-6482."

"That's boring." Raviel tapped her cheek with her finger. "Your new designation is Rivet."

"New designation confirmed," the android replied.

Daeson approached slowly, still keeping his Talon at the ready.

"Sit on this workbench," Raviel said, patting the bench near them. The machine had a hard time lifting itself up on its one good leg to sit on the bench. It was obvious that one of its arms was also nonfunctional.

"Help me," Raviel said to Daeson as she tried to help the android up. It was light, relative to most androids of this size, but still too much for her to lift.

"What are you doing?" Daeson asked. "I hope it's not what I think it is."

Raviel looked over at him and smiled. "He could be useful."

Daeson smirked but gave in and helped Raviel get the android onto the bench.

"Rivet, where will I find replacement parts for you?"

"Inventory location SC-143. I am not authorized to access that location."

Raviel and Daeson searched until they found the location, and before long, Raviel was engrossed with repairing the android. Daeson smiled as he watched her work.

"You really love this, don't you?"

"There is beauty and genius in designs like this. I find it fascinating."

Daeson scrounged for tools that he thought Raviel might find useful, and after three hours of working fervently on the android, it stood before them, fully functional, at least mechanically. Raviel was beaming ear to ear.

"Amazing, Rav. But what if it's not very bright? What if all it can do is sweep and clean a room?"

Raviel began searching the robot's torso and head. "I would love to tap in and look at the code for this thing." She pressed a thumb-sized button on the back of the bot. A panel slid seamlessly away to reveal a beautiful and intricate maze of circuitry and what looked like an input/output port.

"There you are," Raviel said with wonderment. "I think I can use the Starcraft flight processor interface module to tie in."

"You want to bring this thing back to the ship with us?"

"My designation is Rivet," the bot countered.

Daeson shook his head. "Not a good idea, Rav!"

"If it was going to hurt us, it would have already. Like you said, he doesn't seem to be more than a maintenance bot, but if I could access the code and tweak the programming..."

Daeson raised an eyebrow and then nodded.

"Okay, now that makes sense...might be useful after all."

Raviel was clearly pleased. Daeson looked at the bot.

"Rivet, descend the stairs to the lower level," Raviel commanded.

"I am not authorized to leave this sector," the bot replied.

"I am authorizing you to leave this sector," Raviel returned. "From now on you will obey all of our commands. Acknowledge."

The bot's head tilted ever so slightly, which made Daeson's unease return slightly.

"Acknowledged. Please confirm which human will function as my supervisory liege."

"Liege," Daeson repeated. "That's archaic."

Raviel pointed to Daeson. "This human."

The bot looked at Daeson, its hollow eyes scanning his face and torso. Daeson shook his head.

"No—" Daeson began.

"Confirmed," the bot interrupted.

Daeson looked at Raviel; she smirked. The bot turned and moved toward the stairway. Daeson and Raviel followed. Both were amazed at the nimble and skilled movements it made in navigating around fallen obstacles and maneuvering the stairs in particular. Once they reached the street, Daeson took the lead, but shivers flowed up and down his back knowing this ancient machine was following close behind.

The AI bots of the old war had learned well the art of deception from humanity. Their tactics had fooled some of the most brilliant tacticians and led to hundreds of thousands of deaths. What if this thing was deceiving them right now? Daeson kept the bot in his peripheral vision as a precaution.

"Do you really think it's safe?" Daeson looked over at Raviel.

"I'll know for sure once I see his code, but yes, I think so."

Her answer didn't help much. As they walked the silent streets of this ancient city back toward their camp, Daeson had the strange sensation that someone was watching them. He halted Raviel and the bot near what looked like a large transport vehicle that was lying on its side with large sections of its walls ripped away. Daeson concluded that this was one of the vehicles that had travelled on the rail systems he had seen running throughout the city, not dissimilar to their own grav-rail transports.

He scanned the buildings and the vegetation that was reclaiming the city. The silence was eerie, but then again, the entire planet was eerie. His eyes came to rest on the bot—it was staring at him. Chills flowed up and down his spine again. Something about this thing unnerved him. The legends of merciless androids torturing humans for information haunted him.

"What is it, Daeson?" Raviel asked.

Daeson pressed the button to power up his Talon, but before he could bring it to bear on the bot, it lunged for him. In that moment, Daeson realized just how fatal a mistake it had been to allow Raviel to persuade him. He would have little strength to defend himself against such a machine. The bot struck Daeson across his chest, causing him to go flying.

While he was midair, he saw the machine turn instantly about toward Raviel, and his heart sank. Just when it looked as if the machine were about to run her through with its powerful metallic hand, the ground where Daeson had been standing exploded from a plasma discharge. The flying fragments of concrete peppered the back of the bot, protecting Raviel from a deadly barrage of rocky shrapnel.

Daeson smashed into a concrete abutment. Fortunately his impact was somewhat cushioned by a thick viny overgrowth. The air in his lungs nearly left him. He looked upward in the direction from which the plasma blast had come in time to see a horrific site. A large android armed with two Talons jumped from the top of a stone archway just a dozen paces away. It landed with a thud, simultaneously bringing both Talons to bear on Daeson.

A frightful-looking machine with portions of synthetic skin hanging from its face and arms, it was clothed in various fragments of tattered dark clothing. The ribbons of cloth echoed its every move. The thing looked like a walking dead man, yet there was enough facial tissue to convey the full measure of its cold, ruthless heart. If ever there were an angel of death, this machine was it. In the split second that he had, Daeson tried to aim his Talon at the thing, but it would be too late—much too late. There was no cover and no time.

The AI android from an ancient war was clearly obsessed with one more human kill. The machine nearly smiled as it squeezed both triggers of the deadly Talons. But before the plasma charges left the muzzles, Raviel's maintenance bot dove into the side of the AI bot in a crash of metallic fury. The plasma bursts went high, just missing Daeson's head. He rolled for new cover behind a section of the transport.

"Run, Raviel!" he screamed, but his words were muted by the sound of exploding concrete from another Talon blast, this time from a different direction. Another AI metal creature had targeted Raviel. She was already moving, and its shot went wide as she leapt up and over the section of transport to join Daeson. He leveled his Talon on the new AI bot and fired three rounds. Two scored, exploding the bot in a hundred pieces. Daeson and Raviel turned and watched in dazed wonder as their maintenance bot and the first AI bot tangled in a ferocious, robotic hand-to-hand combat, Talons firing every which way in the chaos.

Daeson and Raviel had to duck several times just to keep from being hit. Daeson scanned for more attacking AI bots, but it seemed as if these two were it for now.

"We need to help it!" Raviel exclaimed, mesmerized by the ferocious battle just a few paces away.

Under the cover of the transport section, Daeson took aim, but because he might just as easily hit their bot, he dared not fire. Rivet was clearly taking the brunt of the battle, its limited programming making it incapable of protecting itself from a robotic veteran of combat with perhaps thousands of kills in its memory banks.

Daeson kept them in his sights. At one point the AI bot pinned Rivet beneath him, spun the Talon in its agile metal fingers, and placed the muzzle of it against Rivet's head. Daeson fired at the last split second. He heard Raviel gasp, and in the exploding chaos of metal and smoke, he wondered if he had been too late. When the smoke cleared, atop Rivet sat the headless AI bot, its arm and Talon still in the executionary position. Raviel ran to see if her bot was okay, while Daeson searched the surrounding area once more for additional AI threats.

Raviel carefully moved the AI bot's arm with the powered Talon away from Rivet's head and then pushed the death machine off of him. Rivet lay motionless on the ground.

"Rivet, are you functional?" Raviel asked as Daeson stepped beside her.

Rivet's eyes blinked. He then sat up.

"Yes, I am."

The bot stood and then turned to look at Daeson.

"Are you injured, my liege?"

"What? No," he replied. He circled the bot, amazed at how it had reacted to the AI bot attack. It had saved their lives! He realized that the bot's first reaction had been to save him and not Raviel.

"She is your new liege," he said, pointing at Raviel.

"A liege bond can only be broken by the death of the human or the terminal malfunction of the android," Rivet replied.

Daeson frowned and then looked at Raviel. "Are you okay?"

Raviel glanced up at him and nodded as she began inspecting Rivet for damage. "Remarkable how it reacted to the threat of those AI bots," she said.

Daeson noticed a look on her face that was quite different than one he had seen before. "Yes...what are you thinking?" Daeson asked, as he recovered the three Talons from the remains of the AI bots.

Raviel stayed silent, but she looked concerned. After she was satisfied that her bot was intact, she grabbed Daeson's hand and pulled him away from Rivet.

"Stay here," she commanded over her shoulder.

Daeson handed two of the Talons to Raviel while holstering the other. "They're an old design but obviously just as deadly. If there are two, there may be more, and we need to be ready."

Raviel nodded as she fastened the holsters around her waist. When she was done, she looked up at Daeson. "That thing should not have responded that way." Raviel spoke in hushed tones once they were a few paces away.

"Thing? What happened to 'Rivet'?" Daeson smiled, but Raviel just shook her head. "It saved our lives!" Daeson added. "Who cares what it *should* have done."

Raviel took a deep breath and nodded. "I guess so. Maybe it has some sort of protection algorithm programmed into its maintenance routine in case of manufacturing accidents or something."

"Makes sense."

Raviel looked over at the motionless bot, silently waiting for its next command.

Daeson reached up and gently turned her head toward his with his hand. Her eyes locked in on his, and the concern on her face began to melt away. "I'm just glad you're okay, and if I have to thank a bot for that, I will," he whispered.

She smiled tentatively as the moment lingered.

"Excuse me, my liege." The calm voice of Rivet was right beside them. "Considering the potential of more threats in this vicinity, I recommend we depart at once."

Daeson stopped, irritated.

"He's right," Raviel said quickly as she took a step back. "And that concerns me too."

"Yes...well, let's move on then."

The post-adrenaline rush was beginning to take its toll on Daeson's last reserves of energy, but he knew they didn't have time to rest. After an hour of fast-paced walking, they arrived back at the Starcraft. Daeson was spent. He collapsed under the canopy and only vaguely remembered Raviel giving Rivet the order to sit and remain still. He knew he should stay alert, but he was so utterly exhausted that he was asleep in seconds.

It was Raviel's screams that shattered his slumber. The canopy had collapsed on top of him, and he frantically threw the flimsy material back and forth, trying desperately to free himself while simultaneously feeling for his missing Talons. Raviel's torturous screams tore at his soul. He tried to stand, but the canopy was pinned beneath his knees, and no matter what he did, there seemed no way out. Grabbing the canopy, he searched for a seam and pulled at it with all his might, knowing full well that it was designed to withstand far more force than he could muster.

Raviel's screams were now muted, but her obvious agony was not. In panic he pulled harder on the seam, and it gave just a little; then it split wide open to allow a view of utter horror. Bent over Raviel with metal hands dripping in blood was the maintenance bot. It looked up at Daeson, eyes glowing red with a hatred he did not know could exist.

"Daeson..." He heard Raviel's final gasp.

Suddenly he felt the pull of the canopy wrapped around his arm.

"Daeson!" Slowly the horrific vision melted away into a blurry but peaceful picture of Raviel hovering over him. "Wake up. I need to talk to you."

Daeson shook himself, blinked hard, and rubbed his eyes. The awful images had felt so real. He wrestled to put his emotions in check.

"Thank Omega...you're alright."

Raviel looked confused. "Of course I'm alright. Are you feeling better?"

Daeson scratched his head, trying to quickly forget the images of his nightmare. He looked over at Rivet. Raviel's flight processor interface module was connected to its IO port via an optical cable. The bot appeared to be in a sleep state.

"Yeah. What is it?"

"Something's not right," she said.

"How so?" Daeson asked.

"It took me a while to interpret the code, but—" she hesitated.

"But what?"

"Rivet's code is too simple for it to be able to function like it does."

"Well, there has to be an explanation. Maybe you're not interpreting it properly or perhaps there's an alternate memory it accesses for some of its code."

Raviel nodded. "I thought that too, so I dug further. Come here."

She took Daeson over to the back side of Rivet, where she had removed a larger panel. The inside of the bot was a wonder to behold. Daeson had never seen anything like it. The ancient people of Mesos had to have been brilliant indeed.

"Incredible. Do you understand this?" Daeson asked.

Raviel shrugged. "It's certainly more advanced than what we have, but the functionality of the modules are actually very similar to our own. For instance, this is the—"

Daeson held up his hand. "Don't even try. I skipped Logic Controller Architecture classes for a reason."

Raviel looked disappointed. "Fine, but look here." She pointed to one section of the bot's circuitry that had a crystalline octal component that was pulsing with alternating colors.

"Yes?"

"I don't know what that is," Raviel stated flatly.

Daeson laughed. "Good grief, girl, that's nothing to be concerned about. It's alien!"

Raviel shook her head. "Even though all of this circuitry is alien to me, this one doesn't match the component characteristics of the rest...it's like it's alien to Mesos."

"What do you think it is?" Daeson asked, more intrigued.

"Hyper-processor? Memory? I have no idea. If I'm reading this right, it seems connected to the mobility analytics processor, but I'm only guessing. All I know is that the code I've seen doesn't match its abilities, and that bothers me." She looked up at Daeson. "Maybe you were right. Perhaps we shouldn't have brought it here."

Daeson stood up, walked to the front of the bot, and knelt down on one knee in front of it. He looked over its shoulder at Raviel. "If this thing has some alternative purpose other than what it purports to have, it can't be in regard to us. No one knows we are here, and no other humans have been here since the Omega Star went supernova. It also can't be in support of the AI bots, or we would be dead already. Why would it destroy two AI bots to save us?"

Raviel thought for a moment. "To deceive us so that we would take it off this planet and into the heart of the rest of humanity, where it can restart the AI wars."

Daeson raised both eyebrows. "Wow...that's quite a conspiracy theory," he quipped, but her words sent shivers up and down his spine.

"You know full well that the AI bots' ability to deceive humans was legendary. And this one has had a thousand years to learn more."

Daeson frowned. It was a sobering thought. He replayed Rivet's rescue scene, trying to remember every detail.

"Unplug him," Daeson said before standing and powering up his Talon.

Raviel frowned.

"Just do it...please."

Raviel disconnected the interface module and closed the access panels.

"Rivet, wake up," Daeson commanded.

The bot's eyes opened and looked up at him.

"Why did you save us from the AI bots?"

"You are assigned to me as my liege. My programming mandates that I protect you even at my own destruction."

Daeson glared at the bot as Raviel walked from behind it to stand by Daeson. "That's why you saved me, but why did you save Raviel?"

Slowly Rivet stood. Daeson gripped his Talon a little tighter as the bot looked over toward Raviel.

"I saved the female because I deduced that she was important to you. It is mandated by my programming that I protect all of my liege's assets."

Daeson couldn't stop the ear-to-ear grin that spread across his face.

"Asset!?" Raviel said, fuming. "Asset!?" she nearly yelled, firmly putting her hands on her hips.

Daeson's grin turned into gut-busting laughter. He powered down his Talon and put it back in his holster.

"It stays...I love this thing!" he exclaimed between bursts of laughter.

"I'm going to dismember it bolt by bolt!" Raviel said, grabbing the nearest hyper-wrench.

Daeson grabbed her arm and yanked her toward him. She tried to free herself, but he embraced her from behind, pinning her arms to her side.

"He was just teasing you," Daeson said, trying to quell his laughter, but his words only made her more angry.

"I never tease," Rivet said.

"Shut up, Rivet, if you don't want to end up a bucket of bolts."

Raviel grimaced and tried to throw the wrench at Rivet, but with Daeson's arms now wrapped around her, it just clinked against the bot's leg. Raviel swept Daeson's feet out from under him and laid him on his back. She pounced on him, pinning his arms to the ground. It hurt, but he smiled as he watched her fury grow.

"Do you know how badly I could hurt you right now?" The same fierce fire spewed from her eyes.

"Yes, perhaps, but you are by far the prettiest asset I've ever had." He could tell she wanted to clock him.

She glared down at him. "No one owns me!" Daeson stopped the tease and looked up at this amazing woman, so courageous and full of moxie. "That is one truth of which I have no doubt, Miss Arko."

Raviel's countenance softened. She glanced over at Rivet.

"Any more comments like that and I will cut him apart with a plasma torch, no matter how ingenious his design is."

She looked back at Daeson and caught his admiring eyes. She waited a few more seconds before she started to blush. Then she rolled off of him and began picking up her equipment. Daeson sat up and rubbed a bruised elbow, the result of Raviel's takedown. He wasn't really sure what to think about the bot yet, but he sure liked the girl.

CHAPTER

13

The Dispatch

Over the next few weeks, Daeson grew stronger day by day. He insisted on hand-to-hand combat training and Talon training with Raviel and was duly impressed with her skills. They learned from each other, and Daeson slowly began to feel normal again—actually better than normal. Now that they knew of the potential AI-bot threats, they were extremely careful and prepared when they ventured out from camp and sometimes back into the city.

As Daeson's strength and energy returned, he sensed Raviel withdrawing from him more and more, and it frustrated him. Deep down he knew what it was. A heaviness obscured the bright blue skies of this strange alien world...a heaviness that increased with each passing day...a heaviness that disallowed the hearts of patriots to be free to indulge in the selfish pastime of frivolous affection. She began urging him to return to Jypton now that he had the strength, but when he resisted, it became a source of frequent contention between them. He had little desire to return to a place that no longer held anything for him.

Besides this, there were the dreams. He had never had dreams like these before...so vivid...so real. Every one was so different, except for the one common element—Galeo, the giant moon of Mesos. Each night he awoke more frustrated and confused than on previous nights. It had to have something to do with the Omegeon effects on his body. Would it continue? Would it get worse?

The sun was now settling in between two distant peaks. The orange and red light slowly faded away to reveal the brilliant Omega Nebula in the western sky. So magnificent and so close, Daeson felt as if he could reach out and touch it. It frightened him and drew him at the same time. Raviel sat next to him on a ridge overlooking the majestic reclaimed beauty of Mesos, the silent but always present figure of Rivet not far away. Daeson wanted to move closer to Raviel, but he knew she would retreat. Why must she be so near and so distant at the same time?

"I understand that when Rayleans join with another, it's for life," Daeson said. He glanced at Raviel. "Is this true?"

Raviel flashed a nervous smile without looking at him. "Yes. We are bonded for life."

"Bonded?" Daeson asked.

Raviel nodded. "A man and a woman stand before the clan chieftain or an oracle and are bonded to each other for life. Unlike the Jyptonians, we consider the union of a man and a woman a sacred and lifelong commitment."

Daeson thought of his own parents. Royal unions were expected to appear permanent, but the reality was much different. He remembered being grateful that his mother and father genuinely seemed committed to one another.

"Why?" Daeson asked.

"It is the way of Ell Yon, passed down for thousands of years. There is strength in such a bond, and we cherish it. That's why the man and woman must be compatible in every way."

Raviel glanced up at Daeson as if she were looking for some assurance that he understood what she was saying. He knew exactly what she was saying but remained deadpan. Knowing she thought him "incompatible" hurt. He let the sunset soothe the moment, taken by its beauty. At times he wished he didn't care for Raviel, but he did, and nothing seemed to move his heart away from that.

"What if we never go back?" he asked quietly.

After a few seconds of silence, she nodded. "Tempting, isn't it?" she replied. The response surprised him.

"We have a whole new world just to ourselves," Daeson said. "Jypton probably doesn't even know we're gone. After all, what difference could the two of us make?"

"From here it's hard to imagine any difference at all," she said. "But—"

"There is no 'but,' Rav. If the Plexus in all of its technology and intellect can't change a thing, then what could we possibly do? If we go back, we die."

Raviel turned and looked over at him. "It's not about us."

"It could be," Daeson countered.

He sensed that familiar fire rising up in her again.

"You just don't get it, do you?"

"What I don't get is you! I felt closer to you when I was a Jyptonian prince and you were a lowly Drudge. Why?"

Her eyes grew fierce. "Because of this...this right here! After everything you've seen, you still don't believe in any of it, do you?"

Daeson shook his head. "The truth is I haven't *seen* anything that corroborates any of your beliefs." Daeson chose to ignore his previous hallucinatory vision of Ell Yon. "No one has ever seen these mythical Immortals you speak of. We became sick here on Mesos because of Omegeon radiation poisoning, and Deitum Prime still has way more evidence of being good for us than the evil, mind-controlling, diabolical substance you claim it to be. And as far as the Rayleans go, they are just the recipients of the unfortunate circumstance of being under the influence of a far superior power who is exploiting them to their advantage. It has happened to many people throughout time, all across the galaxy. We have a chance at a new beginning here."

Raviel didn't move her hard gaze from Daeson. He took a deep breath, trying to find the right tone for his next words. What did he have to lose? He seemed to be losing her more with each passing day.

"Regardless of what you believe or what I believe, I...I..."

"Don't!" Raviel said and looked away.

Daeson's frustration peaked. Now he was embarrassed for even trying to share his feelings.

"So we don't believe the same things. How much does it really matter?"

Slowly she turned and looked into Daeson's eyes with a sadness that tore at his soul. "It matters everything," she whispered. "People are dying. My people...*your* people! The principles we believe in matter the most—principles that compel people to die for them. Over the last one hundred years, the Plexus has carefully positioned itself so that when the opportunity arose, they would be ready to take advantage of it. You, Daeson Starlore, are that opportunity. The Plexus needs you! The Plexus is our hope for freedom!"

Daeson clenched his teeth. "If that is true, then where is your mighty Ell Yon in all of this? Why is your hope in the Plexus and not in him? Listen, there is nothing—and I mean nothing— that I could do for the Plexus or for any Raylean for that matter. Look what I did to you."

"Nothing? Really? You saved my life. You were trained in the royal house of Lockridge," Raviel countered. "You're a skilled pilot and warrior. You know the inner workings of the Jyptonian government. That's something we've never had before. I believe you are in this position, at this time, for this purpose. Don't you remember what Sabella the oracle told you—that you were destined to turn sorrow into joy for many people?"

Daeson had nearly forgotten the white-haired woman and her cryptic words.

"That's when I started believing...started hoping again."

Daeson cringed at the thought. "I'm not that guy, Raviel. Besides, it would take a lot more than just some great leader. It would take an armada! Jypton is one of the wealthiest and most fortified planets in this sector of the galaxy. Your thinking is just crazy!"

"Yes, but those forces are designed to protect them from invaders outside the planet, not from a rebellion within," Raviel protested.

"Those same forces would easily squash an uprising before it begins," Daeson rebutted.

Raviel pulled her knees up to her chest and looked out across the alien landscape. Galeo was now bright and full as it raced across the southern sky.

"So the Rayleans are just supposed to bow their heads in subjugation forever."

"If the alternative is death, which would you choose for them? Because they will most certainly all die—or at least enough of them to make sure this never happens again." Daeson thought of Linden's stone face the last time they met.

Raviel looked up and over at Daeson once more, the ember of her fiery spirit still evident. "Everyone who dies fighting for the freedom of their people dies a hero. Those who turn their backs on such a noble cause live as cowards...no matter the odds." She stood and took a few seconds to look down at him, disappointment spilling all over him. "I could never love a coward."

Then she turned and walked away, but her words lingered, cutting deep.

That hot-headed, arrogant woman! The words nearly left his lips. Clearly there was no future with her. He picked up a small stone and threw it. "Well, that went well," he muttered.

"I think not..." Rivet's soothing voice rattled him. The forgotten bot was just a few paces away, staring at him "...Master Daeson," the bot finished.

Daeson stood and went to Rivet. He squinted and looked the bot up and down, feeling mocked by the machine.

"Maintenance bot indeed!" Daeson smirked and then looked back out to the night sky. He took a few deep breaths to assuage his anger and was once more taken with the majestic form of the orange lantern called Galeo, the light that was never quenched.

Come to me.

The whisper nearly haunted him. He'd had thoughts that did not seem to be his own in the past, but those had all stopped since coming to Mesos. Though not his own, this thought was different. Why did he feel inexplicably drawn to Galeo? Every day he remained on Mesos, the thought grew stronger, and now...more thoughts that were not his own. What was happening?

Daeson shook himself and began walking back to camp. Rivet turned and followed. He was not in a hurry to rejoin Raviel, but in spite of his anger and resentment, leaving her alone always made him nervous.

Raviel couldn't ever remember feeling this angry after just a conversation...angry and sad. She was frustrated beyond words. Oftentimes she had conversations regarding Ell Yon and the Immortals with people that were just as diametrically opposed, but she had been able to walk away remaining relatively calm. Somehow with Daeson, it was different. At first she had attributed it to the fact that his potential influence on their plight could be significant. She wanted him to believe so he could join their cause, but deep down she knew it was more than even that. She cared for him. From the beginning she'd tried not to, but her feelings would not leave her alone.

Many young Raylean men had expressed interest in her in the past. She'd been told that she had her mother's natural beauty and her father's charm, which she reasoned was why they were drawn to her. But her life at the time was too serious to be caught up in the frivolous pursuits of love and all of the silliness and complications that went with it. She reasoned she would have time for it later. Thus, it had been easy to reject them all. For some inexplicable reason, that had not been the case with Daeson Lockridge.

She remembered her first encounter with him and how it had jarred her emotional fortress. It was just a tremor, but it shook her. And ever since, their lives had become entangled because of her mission as a Plexus spy. It frustrated her...toyed with her...teased her. She desperately wanted her stable, focused life back, but now by this sequence of bizarre events, she was stranded on a planet with the one guy that messed with her heart.

Halfway back to the camp, she stopped and looked up at the stars through the red blossoms of the beautiful trees surrounding her. She closed her eyes and took a deep breath.

"What is happening to me?" she pleaded. Every direction she turned, she felt hemmed in—by the Jyptonians, by Daeson, by this planet. Her mind turned back to Daeson, and she resumed her walk back to camp.

"There is no reason whatsoever to have feelings for this guy," she voiced to herself. Perhaps saying it out loud would make it true. "Except for the fact that he is handsome, charming, skilled, and clearly an amazing Starcraft pilot...that's all. No other reason!" She shook her head. "What's wrong with you, Raviel? You're acting like schoolgirl! Pull yourself together!"

She easily dismissed the attributes about him that other girls would be wooed by, but she knew there was something more—something deep and undiscovered that drew her to him.

She slowed her gait so she could finish her conversation before she arrived at camp. With the light of Galeo now shining brightly and invading the dark of night, she could now see the camp ahead.

"You can't love him. He refuses to accept the truth of Ell Yon, even though it is all around him." She stopped and put a hand on a nearby tree. Her head lowered. "And he will never be as close to the truth as he is right now. He doesn't even yet accept the fact that he is Raylean."

Raviel's sadness deepened. She killed her feelings for him once more, knowing that eventually one day those feelings might never revive.

"But at what cost, Raviel?" She resumed her walk to camp. If she truly were successful in rejecting her feelings for this man, she knew she would never be able to love again. There would be no one else that stirred her soul like he did.

"So be it!" she said with clenched fists, forsaking her emotions for a higher call once and for all.

When she arrived back at camp, something was different. She froze, noticing a subtle green pulsating light, and her heart quickened.

CHAPTER

14

Revolution!

"**D**aeson!"

Daeson was halfway to the camp when he heard her call for help. He drew his Talon and charged it, sprinting as fast as he could back to the Starcraft. Rivet was right beside him. "Shall I go ahead?" Rivet asked.

Daeson grimaced. "Yes…of course…protect her!"

Rivet quickly outdistanced Daeson in their race to reach her. When Daeson arrived, Rivet was standing guard, scanning the perimeter of the camp, his back to Raviel. Raviel was kneeling at the base of the Starcraft, her glass tablet glowing in the dark. Next to her the quantum entanglement communicator was pulsing subtle amber lights about its periphery. She looked up at Daeson, horror upon her face. Daeson knelt down in front of her.

"What is it, Rav? What's wrong?"

She slowly handed the glass tablet to him, unable to speak.

Encoded communiqué six alpha bravo bravo four. Agent thirty-two. Final transmission…

"It just started receiving...it's over...they're all..." Raviel muttered. Daeson heard her in between reading what was on the glass.

Do not attempt to contact. This is a priority one transmission. Plexus has been compromised. Destroy all devices and material. Global executions commencing. End transmission.

"What...what does it mean?" Daeson asked.

Raviel stared blankly at him.

"It's over. The Plexus is gone. This kind of transmission is only sent when..." Raviel swallowed hard. "When the entire network has been compromised."

She looked up at him. "Daeson, they're killing everyone!"

Daeson dared not speak. He put a gentle hand on her shoulder.

"They won't stop at the Plexus. They won't stop until every last Raylean with any association is dead."

Daeson's thoughts turned to Linden and his father. Raviel was right. If Linden's investigation of the secret Raylean intelligence at the academy had led to a full discovery of the Plexus, then Marcus Lockridge and the ruling Elite would be ruthless in eliminating them. Anger swelled inside him.

"All hope is lost," Raviel whispered. "If only we had been there."

"If we had been there, we would be dead too," he said tenderly.

Her eyes fell dark. The fire was gone.

"But we *are* still alive, and you were right. We must try—it's time to go back."

Raviel looked empty. "It's too late. We're too late."

It took two days to recover and prepare for their flight home. After lengthy discussions away from Rivet, they decided to bring the android with them.

"How compact can you make yourself, Rivet?" Daeson asked.

Daeson and Raviel watched in amazement as Rivet folded himself up into a rectangular box shape the size of a hand-carried case, albeit much heavier. But the transformation was astounding.

They hoisted the droid up into a small cargo bay near the back of the Starcraft and were soon strapping themselves in. Before firing up the engines, Daeson took a moment to look one last time at this ancient alien world that had saved them and nearly killed them at the same time.

"What an unusual place this is," Daeson said through the com link.

"Yes," came Raviel's sober reply.

Raviel was different now. The spark of life so typical of her had vanished ever since she had received the dispatch. It jarred him, and with every passing hour, his conviction grew until he had become keenly aware of his ugly, selfish heart. No wonder she had withdrawn from him. She had seen this coming, and he had refused to believe her. Embarrassed and humiliated, the anticipation and dread of returning to Jypton was anguishing, but he knew it was what they had to do. If any of this was truly his fault, he needed to face up to it.

Daeson powered up the engines, performed his preflight checks, and lifted off. Within a few moments, they were escaping the atmosphere of Mesos and navigating back toward the slipstream conduit. The Omegeon radiation was high, but now its effects didn't feel life-threatening. Something inside Daeson was changing, and he didn't understand it just yet.

After the conduit jump, Daeson carefully navigated to approach Jypton under cover of the sun and its other orbiting planets. Their final approach to Jypton was remarkably uneventful, as if the entire planet were distracted.

"Where to, Raviel?" Daeson asked.

"I want to go home," Raviel replied, "but the place we will find answers is at the Plexus secret camp if it hasn't yet been discovered."

"Good call. Chances of getting anywhere near Athlone will be slim."

Daeson entered Jypton's atmosphere over the western ocean and flew just feet from the surface to foil any detection stations. Raviel fed him coordinates for the Plexus rebel camp, but it wasn't necessary. As they made landfall, the fury of a bloody battle spilled flames and fumes into the air. Here in a remote region of Jypton was the last stand of an insignificant race of people, desperate for a chance at freedom.

"Oh, no!" Raviel's voice whispered through the com link.

A flight of six Starcrafts were raining fire down on a line of Raylean rebels from above, while grav-tanks and foot soldiers bombarded fortifications on the ground.

"It's a massacre, Daeson. We have to do something!"

Both fuel tanks were already low. He calculated he had about ten minutes of combat time.

"We can take out one or two of the Starcraft quickly, but then—" He didn't need to finish. Raviel would know that their chance of survival was minimal against such odds.

Daeson flew low to the ground in a wide arc to engage from behind the Jyptonian forces. Just as he targeted one of the Starcraft, a plasma burst exploded its right engine, sending it pitching wildly into the ground. The resulting explosion scattered steel and fuel across the battlefront, taking out one of the Jyptonian grav-tanks. Daeson turned to see that the shot had come from an identical Starcraft.

"What just happened?" Raviel asked.

"I have no idea," Daeson said, targeting a second Starcraft while keeping an eye on the one that had made the first shot. He locked on, fired three bursts, and then pulled up to avoid the expanding debris caused by the explosion. He glanced toward his potential ally and watched as it targeted another Jyptonian Starcraft, but within seconds he had picked up a tail and was in trouble. Daeson pulled off his second target, locked on to his ally's tail, and fired. It took two tries, but he finally made the hit.

Whoever was flying his ally's Starcraft seemed to immediately understand the unspoken pact. They quickly worked together to target and eliminate the remaining four Starcrafts. Much of their success was due to the surprise and shock caused by the Jyptonians' being attacked by Starcrafts that they had assumed were friendly.

With the air threat temporarily eliminated, Daeson and the ally ship began targeting Jyptonian grav-tanks and ground soldiers. The resulting turn in the battle was dramatic. The Jyptonian forces began retreating in mass, and the remaining Raylean rebel forces sent volley after volley of plasma cannon bursts after them.

Daeson's Starcraft was now flashing a low fuel warning—he was flying on fumes and needed to set down immediately. As he flew across the frontline toward the Rayleans looking for a landing site, the ally Starcraft came up beside him, dipped its wings, and then flew ahead. Daeson followed. Sixty seconds later both Starcrafts were settling into an open field just behind Raylean lines.

Daeson shut down the engines, raised the canopy, and jumped to the ground. He looked up at the pilot exiting the other Starcraft, wondering who had dared fight for the Rayleans in a Jyptonian Starcraft. The pilot jumped to the ground and lifted his helmet.

"Tig!" Daeson yelled with a wide smile.

"By Omega, I can't believe it's you, Master Lockridge!" Tig said, returning the grin.

Daeson grabbed Tig and hugged him. "Thank the stars you were up there. I thought that was going to be my last flight!"

Raviel came to stand by Daeson.

"You remember Raviel?"

Raviel stuck out her hand, but Tig bowed, and Raviel didn't know quite what to do. She glanced toward Daeson and then back to Tig.

"Daeson told me what you did to save me," Raviel said, stepping toward Tig. She gave him a hug and backed away. "I don't know how I can thank you."

Tig seemed surprised and a little flustered by Raviel's actions. "I was grateful to do it, my lady."

"I'm no lady, sir...just a Raylean mechtech," Raviel corrected.

Tig smiled. "If you are the lady of Master Lockridge, you are a lady to me as well."

Raviel blushed, clearly not used to such devotion or to such association to Daeson.

Thump, thump, thump.

Tig tilted his head at the sound and looked toward Daeson's Starcraft.

"Ah, Rav would you let Rivet out of the cargo bay?"

Raviel walked to the underside of the Starcraft and operated the release mechanism to open the cargo bay. As the door slid open, a metal cube fell to the ground. Tig walked toward it.

"What in the galaxy is—" he began, but then Rivet began to unfold. In just a few seconds, the android was standing upright. Tig walked around the android, exchanging glances with Daeson.

"You must have quite the story to tell. I've no idea where you acquired this droid, but it looks to me like it's close to violating the AI restrictions. Have you tested it?"

"I've downloaded the code. It's clean," Raviel said with a quick glance toward Daeson.

Her explanation seemed to satisfy Tig.

"Well, I'm pretty sure we don't have long until the next wave," Tig stated, looking at Daeson.

"Yes," Daeson replied. "We surprised them once, but the next attack will probably be an entire squadron. We need to warn the Rayleans. Once the Jyptonians organize, there'll be no stopping them."

After a short hike across rough terrain, they walked into a scene of chaos. Dead and wounded lay everywhere. Scorched earth and equipment littered the battle zone. Searching through the area, they found a young man giving orders and were taken to the crude rudiments of a field headquarters. Even in the chaos, Daeson and Tig both could see that there was little organization to what was happening. This was a rebellion without leadership and resources. Daeson felt the overwhelming cloud of futility and defeat everywhere.

Beneath a camouflaged tent, two men and a woman were in a heated debate over their next move.

"Where do we go? For what do we wait?" A broad, dark-haired man swiped a large glass on the table they were bent over, which showed their position, remaining personnel, and weapons. Daeson thought he looked familiar.

"Agreed," said the woman. "We stand and fight now! There is no tomorrow. Better to die fighting than in an execution."

"They are massing an attack on a scale that will obliterate us in seconds...it's suicide," the second man argued.

"He's right," Daeson agreed, approaching the gathering. "You won't survive."

His comment immediately garnered the attention of all three. They looked up from the table, eyes weary and worn.

"Trisk!" Raviel exclaimed, rushing to him.

The dark-haired man was slow to react.

"Raviel?"

"Yes...yes it's me!"

He held her at arms-length and then embraced her. "You're alive! We only heard rumors."

He looked up at Daeson, his eyes slowly filling with fury. Pushing Raviel aside, Trisk went to him. Daeson swallowed, his hand instinctively gliding over his Talon. Daeson hesitated; Trisk, however, did not. He grabbed Daeson and threw him up against a stack of containers. Tig grabbed Trisk's shoulders, but one quick punch put Tig on the ground.

"Stop!" Raviel shouted, as Trisk brought a shortened Talon to Daeson's throat.

"You brought this on our people!"

Now fully recovered, Daeson considered a counter-move but quickly dismissed it. If he was going to be any use, it would not come from attacking one of their commanders. He remained firmly in Trisk's powerful grasp. The man clenched his teeth as he pressed the blade against Daeson's neck. The stasis field was off, or Daeson would have already been sliced through.

Raviel grabbed Trisk's hand that was threatening to cut through his throat.

"Stop, Trisk!" Raviel shouted.

"Why should I? He's responsible for the deaths of thousands of Rayleans throughout Jypton."

Daeson heard a Talon charge.

"Let him go," Tig ordered, his Talon pointed at Trisk's head.

Two more Talons charged, both pointed at Tig.

Rivet stood silently in the background. He might as well have been a wall decoration.

"These men risked their lives piloting those Starcrafts," Raviel exclaimed.

"It's only delayed the inevitable," Trisk growled.

"He saved my life, Trisk," Raviel pleaded. "He risked his own to save me."

Daeson felt the hatred in the man and wondered if this was the end. Trisk sneered, but Daeson felt the grip on his neck lessen and heard the blade of the Talon retract.

Carefully, slowly, the other three Talons all lowered and powered down. Weapons withdrawn but not holstered, the tension abated somewhat. Trisk's face contorted as he retreated in silence, while Daeson felt his throat, thankful it was still whole. Raviel quickly stepped between them but stayed close to Daeson, as Trisk walked back to the table, leaned over it, and hung his head.

"What happened here, Trisk?" Raviel asked.

The other woman in the group looked incredulous. "What happened? Have you been hiding under a rock?"

"We were marooned on another planet until today," she replied. Daeson noticed she deliberately didn't mention Mesos, knowing it would raise a thousand questions they didn't have time to answer.

Trisk slowly looked up at them, eyes still fierce.

"Once *he* disappeared," Trisk nodded toward Daeson, "the Jyptonians unleashed the fires of Gehenna on Rayleans everywhere. They claimed he was a spy and began hunting for both of you."

"Somehow they knew who belonged to the Plexus," the other man added. "They executed all of them and anyone else that was remotely associated with them."

Raviel turned to Trisk, "My parents?"

Trisk looked blankly at her. "I don't know. I haven't heard from them, but...," Trisk began and then shook his head. He didn't finish. Raviel put her hand to her mouth. Daeson tried to imagine the horror of it, closing his eyes as the images filled his mind.

"The Plexus is gone," Trisk said. He stood straight and held out his arms. "We are all that's left of the rebellion. And now they will hunt us down until all that remains are the scorched bones of those who believed in freedom."

Solemn seconds of silence passed.

"You need to retreat," Daeson finally said.

"To where?" the woman questioned, her voice thick with indignation.

Daeson stepped forward.

"Anywhere," Daeson replied. "If you stay and fight, you will all die! You must live to fight another day...a day when there is hope."

"Says the Prince of Jypton!" Trisk scowled. "We have no hope, Jyptonian. You took that from us every single day you lived in your ivory tower."

Raviel stepped forward. "He's not Jyptonian—he's Raylean just like you and me."

"He's Jyptonian to me!" Trisk rebuked.

"We saw transports on the way here. Do you have enough to get your forces out of here?" Tig asked.

"Perhaps," the other man responded. "And we do have multiple retreat points. If we could just get beyond visual range, our jammers could mask our retreat, but we won't have enough time."

"I'll make sure you do," Daeson said. He looked at Trisk and the other two commanders.

"I am detecting communication from the Jyptonian forces," Rivet's voice interrupted. They all turned to look at the bot. A short antenna had extended upward from one side of the bot's head. "Thirty Starcrafts and a division of ground forces are being mobilized."

Daeson looked at Raviel. She seemed as surprised as he.

"Every second we wait, our chance of survival decreases," the other man petitioned Trisk and the woman.

Trisk and the woman commander looked at each other, finally nodding in agreement.

"Call for the evacuation, and we'll provide cover with the Starcrafts." Daeson turned to face Tig and Rivet. "Let's go."

Daeson heard the Raylean leaders order the plasma cannons to be set on auto-defense and for all mines to be armed and set.

Daeson, Raviel, Tig, and Rivet set out back to the Starcrafts, making plans as they went.

"I don't think your cousin likes me much," Daeson acknowledged as they walked briskly to where they had set down.

"Trisk is a good man. If you can win his trust, he would fight a Kolazo beast for you."

"That first night I met him...the night we danced, did he know what you were doing?" Daeson asked.

"No. I was part of the Plexus secret intelligence, but he was part of the armed resistance. None of my friends or family knew I was involved."

"What's the plan, boss?" Tig asked.

They had to navigate around a transport that was just setting down.

"Yes...what is the plan? Our Starcraft has no fuel," Raviel reminded. "And besides, what could two Starcrafts do against an entire Jyptonian squadron?"

Daeson looked over at Tig. "I need your ship one more time."

Tig nodded. "The tanks are at seventy-five percent."

"Good. First we'll get airborne and transfer enough fuel into the other Starcraft so you can provide cover for the retreating transports. I'll buy you time by disrupting the attack."

Tig glanced back and forth between Daeson and Raviel.

"That's suicide," Tig said. "Surely with two of us attacking together, at least—"

"No," Daeson cut him off. "I need you to take Raviel and lead the retreat. They need you...both of you."

"Excuse me, but that's not happening," Raviel shot back. "If you think for one minute that I am going to let you fly a suicide mission alone, you can forget it. I'm coming with you!"

"I don't plan on engaging the whole squadron—just distracting them to buy you some time. Believe me, I have no plans to die today."

Raviel glared at him, but Daeson ignored her. A few seconds later they arrived at the Starcrafts, and Tig took immediately to prepping them.

Daeson grabbed Raviel by the arm and pulled her away a few feet.

"I know you don't like this, but it's the only way. Didn't we come here to help them?"

She started to protest, but Daeson continued. "If I don't rejoin with you right away, transmit your coordinates when you're safe. I'll catch up with you once this is over."

"You better!" Raviel glared at him, her eyes reddened. "What I said back on Mesos...I didn't mean—"

Daeson put two fingers to her lips. "It's okay...trust me," he said with confidence and a smirk, knowing there was the very real possibility they would never see each other again. Raviel bit her lip and quickly turned away toward Rivet.

"Take him."

"What good will that do?" Daeson asked. "He'll be more useful to you."

"I need to know someone is with you, even if it is a strange old bot."

She looked at Rivet. "You keep him alive, you old bucket of bolts!" she ordered.

"I will do my best, my lady," Rivet replied.

Raviel shook her head, ever perplexed by the bot.

Daeson went to Tig and grabbed his shoulder.

"Take care of her, Tig."

"With my life, Master—"

Daeson held up his hand. "No, Tig. Here, I'm just Daeson."

"With my life," Tig finished.

Daeson helped Raviel strap in and then quickly made his way to his own Starcraft.

"Fold up, Rivet," Daeson said.

"I can be more useful to you in the second cockpit," Rivet said.

Daeson imagined the bot's metal arms and legs flailing about during combat.

"I don't think so. Fold up."

Rivet hesitated, which caused Daeson to raise an eyebrow.

"My liege, my ocular acuity is 436 times better than yours. My ability to process information and forecast probabilities will be invaluable as you encounter overwhelming odds. Additionally, since you are planning to attempt to secretly rejoin their fleet as you did before, they will have undoubtedly encrypted their transponder codes to prevent such an attack, and my ability to decrypt and transmit the proper code will give you the single opportunity you have of surviving, a chance that is currently one hundred twelve to one." Rivet tilted his head toward Daeson.

Daeson looked at the bot, dumbfounded. Surely this was more than a maintenance bot. Whatever it was, he would have to figure it out later.

"In the back seat," he ordered.

Daeson jumped in the front cockpit and strapped in. He was delighted to see fuel tanks that were nearly full. Daeson fired up the engines and launched. Within a few seconds he had dropped his air-to-air fuel transfer boom and Tig connected.

"I'll transfer twenty percent. That should give you enough to cover the retreat."

"Check," Tig replied.

Two minutes later Tig disconnected, and Daeson was flying a wide arc around the battlefront.

"Your best approach is from the southeast at a heading of three six point four. There is enough terrain elevation to mask our approach." Rivet offered.

"I'll ask for input when I need it," Daeson barked. He scanned his map and displays to find that the bot was dead on.

Daeson double-checked to make sure his transponder was not transmitting.

"If you do not transmit a transponder code, they will immediately target you as an enemy." Rivet offered again.

"Can you decipher their encrypted codes and transmit one that will work?" Daeson asked.

"I am working on deciphering their command network now."

Daeson marveled. This machine was becoming scary smart.

"What are you?" Daeson couldn't help the question.

"I am an RI-6482 maintenance android. I was designed to communicate and adapt to a variety of operations, based on the environment within which I operate. I am merely functioning to maximize my capabilities in this new environment and to help my liege. Should I continue?"

Daeson tried to imagine a race of people that had the ability to build and program such a bot.

"Yes...continue—and quickly."

Daeson picked up the squadron in its attack formation. He had three minutes tops if he were going to help the Rayleans at all.

"Complete. If you have the piloting skills to stealthily join the formation, our transponder code should be accepted," Rivet reported.

Daeson scowled. "Did you just ridicule me?"

"I do not understand the question."

Daeson shook his head. He scanned the com channels until he found the same one the squadron was communicating on and then dropped his Starcraft low to the horizon, looking for just the right opportunity to rejoin the forming squadron of Jyptonian A-32 Starcrafts. The urgency and chaos of organizing such an attack force gave Daeson just the distraction he needed to rejoin on the wing of two launching Starcrafts. Before long he was in position with thirty other Starcrafts. Evidently, Rivet's transponder code was working.

Daeson looked beneath them and saw the division of ground forces already moving toward the Raylean camp. It was frightening to behold. He could imagine Linden watching every move of the Jyptonian forces with thirsty anticipation. Daeson had seen the awakening of a future cold-hearted despot in Linden that transcended even the evil of his father. On the day Raviel was arrested, Daeson had gotten a glimpse into the heart of a man who had tasted power, and it was dreadful. It was almost as if Linden had a destiny with tyranny. The day Linden ruled Jypton would be a grim day indeed.

Daeson scanned the space around him and considered his next move. His heart began to race. The truth was that his chances of surviving this were as minimal as Rivet's prediction. Once Daeson opened fire, he probably wouldn't last more than a couple of minutes. He hoped he could take out two or three Starcrafts and then draw a few away from the assault.

"This is a bad plan." Rivet's voice held an edge of disdain. It made Daeson angry. What would an android understand about strategy and sacrifice?

"And you have a better one?"

Daeson took a breath and armed up his energy weapons. "Yes, actually. Now that I have access to the command network, I can force other Starcrafts to transmit false transponder codes, which will flag them as potential enemies."

Daeson froze. "Rivet, that's brilliant! Do it!"

"Transmitting false codes now."

The com channel immediately went nuts as Command Central issued alerts to the Starcraft commanders. Some of the Starcrafts began breaking formation. Daeson targeted one and fired. The resulting fur ball was unlike anything Daeson had ever seen before. Within seconds, thirty Starcrafts were wrapped up in an air-to-air combat frenzy, much like two wild cats trying to kill each other.

Daeson dropped out of the chaos and made a lateral attack on the advancing division below. Other Starcrafts followed him, but some of those were transmitting false codes, so ground forces began firing on them. Soon the entire Jyptonian attack force was in a ferocious battle against itself. The auto defense plasma cannons of the Rayleans added to the bombardment, and any grav-tanks that got too close to the frontline hit mines.

Rivet bombarded the alert channels with bogus commands that compounded and prolonged the confusion. When it was apparent that the destruction of the air and land forces was self-perpetuating, Daeson bugged out low and to the north. When he caught sight of the Raylean retreat, he switched over to Tig's secure com channel.

"Phantom Two, this is Phantom One. Come in," Daeson called out.

"Phantom One, check. What did you do back there?" Tig radioed back. "Looks like you singlehandedly took out the whole attack force!"

Raviel jumped on. "Are you okay?"

Daeson pulled up next to Tig and Raviel. She dropped her visor and looked his way.

"Roger that. I had a little help from your old bucket of bolts."

Daeson quickly scanned the retreating transport ships. They had begun scattering in dozens of directions. "I'll provide cover to the east. You two cover transports moving North. Just a few more minutes, and they should be in the clear. After that, they're on their own."

"Check," Tig replied.

A few minutes later Daeson rejoined with Tig in close finger-tip formation. Daeson knew what Raviel would hope for next.

"Tig, we need to get back to Athlone," he radioed.

There was a long pause.

"I'm not so sure that's a good idea," Tig replied. "Security in and out of the city is extremely tight, and you're not going to like what you see."

"That doesn't matter; we must go there."

Daeson knew Tig was calculating the risks—not for himself, but for Daeson and Raviel.

"Please." Raviel's one-word plea overpowered any calculation of risk.

"It will take a couple of days, but I know a way. Follow me," Tig responded as his Starcraft banked steeply to the left, pulling up and away. Daeson followed.

CHAPTER

15

Turning Point

Tig and Daeson set down their Starcrafts near a remote farm west of Hydon, a small Jyptonian city. "My father has been helping a few Rayleans develop an underground transportation network to get people in jeopardy out of Athlone, but it's possible we could use his network to get you two back into the city as well."

"Your father?" Daeson asked.

Tig looked concerned.

"We have a contingency plan. We knew the day might come where either he or I would be discovered. When I saw you target that flight of Starcrafts, I knew the day had come." Tig looked down at the ground. "I've sent word to my father...I just hope he gets it in time."

Daeson put a hand on Tig's shoulder. "Your father sounds like a very resourceful man. I'm sure he's okay."

Tig nodded. They were standing in a large building used to store harvested crops.

"You need to be prepared for what you're going to see in Drudgetown," Tig said as they waited for a contact to arrive, evidently the first of many, for they were still far away from Athlone.

Daeson and Raviel waited anxiously.

"The sentries have been merciless. Even the ground forces were called in on some of the assaults."

"Assaults?" Raviel's eyes were wide. "Why?"

"You have no idea what happened after you left, do you?"

"No, we don't," Daeson said, glancing toward Raviel. "What happened?"

Tig took a deep breath.

"Things escalated quickly. Once they figured out that you used a Starcraft to assault four sentries and rescue Raviel, there was retribution on all Rayleans in Athlone. Perhaps it was just an excuse, but like Trisk said, they suspected that you might come back, so they began hunting you, and in the process many Rayleans were tortured and killed.

"This sparked retaliation by the Plexus and the underground rebel forces. Within two weeks, the Raylean rebels were conducting assaults, and in the process, members of the Plexus were discovered. The persecution and retribution quickly spread to the other cities, and before long the entire planet was in chaos. In a desperate attempt to strike a crippling blow to the Royals...," Tig paused and looked at Daeson before continuing, "...the Plexus, along with the underground forces, orchestrated an assassination attempt on Chancellor Lockridge."

Daeson's eyes widened. "What? Assassination?"

Tig nodded. "And they succeeded."

Raviel gasped as she grabbed Daeson's arm. His heart nearly stopped. He felt pain for Linden, even as he imagined how Linden's rage at such an act would propel the transformation of the man into a tyrant. Daeson's eyes closed as he realized that any kindness or mercy left in Linden would now be burned to ashes. His childhood brother was truly gone.

"Linden Lockridge is now the Chancellor of Jypton, so you can imagine the fury that was unleashed on Rayleans everywhere because of what happened. This is the darkest age the planet has ever known. All of the Drudgetowns look like war zones. Public executions are conducted almost weekly as they purge the Raylean people of all resistance. The Jyptonian forces are merciless because of the assassination."

Daeson stumbled to a bale of hay and sat down, his hands covering a face of sorrow. What had he done? Tears swelled in his eyes and fell between his fingers. The burden was too great...too personal.

"Is there any chance that my parents survived?" Raviel pleaded.

Tig pursed his lips.

"I don't know. My father and I and a few other sympathetic Jyptonians helped get as many Rayleans out of Drudgetown as possible, at least those that were at great risk. There are a dozen secret refugee camps around the planet. Anyone associated with you was obviously a prime target after the assassination, but I never got word if your parents made it out or not. I'm sorry, my lady."

Daeson slowly lifted his head to look at Tig.

"And my mother? What has Linden done with her?"

He could only imagine how far Linden would go to quench his thirst for revenge, especially if he already knew that Daeson was actually Raylean.

"My father told me that she was taken to Austerbach Manor, but no one knows for sure."

Occasionally the Royals and sometimes the Elite concealed individuals that were an embarrassment to the prestigious reputation of their order. It was customary neither to reject them to a lower caste nor place them in positions of influence, so they were harbored at Austerbach Manor. Essentially it was a guarded prison of measured luxury that one rarely was released from. Daeson, like Raviel, was condemned to endure the anxiety of the indeterminate fate of his loved ones.

"I'm sorry, Master Daeson, there was nothing we could do."

Daeson looked up at Tig.

"You and your father have already done so much and at such risk." He shook his head. "How can we ever repay you?"

"I only wish we could do more."

After three days of careful and clandestine movement and with help from the brave souls that formed the Raylean underground transport, Daeson and Raviel found themselves standing on the edge of Drudgetown. The visual was utterly depressing. Daeson felt the heavy hand of oppression hanging in the air everywhere he looked. Many buildings were in shambles, the smoke of recent assaults rising up like flags of submission. Streets were littered with trash, debris, and destroyed grav-vehicles.

"Tig was right; it looks like a war zone." Raviel's words were almost imperceptible.

Daeson chanced a glance her direction, her cheeks moist with tears. There was an undeniable ownership of this devastation that he could not escape. Guilt choked him—guilt through his association as one of the royal family and guilt through the catalytic sequence of devastation as a result of his fleeing the planet. Was this death and destruction truly of his doing?

They moved numbly through the streets, absorbing the full measure of the oppression meted out by the powers of Jypton. When they arrived at Raviel's home, shattered memories lay everywhere. Standing in the middle of the ravaged dwelling, Raviel slowly sank to the floor. She clutched her bosom, sobbing heavily at evidence she knew no one would dare to acknowledge. Daeson knelt down and wrapped his arms around her. In silence he held her until she could stay no more.

They found a makeshift shelter, where a few noble Rayleans were feebly trying to feed and care for the wounded of Drudgetown. They joined in, trying to help in any way possible, but there was such a void of food and shelter. The scene was crushing to Daeson's heart, and he knew that Raviel probably felt it even more intensely. In the corner, an eight-year-old girl sat silently rocking back and forth, staring at nothing. Raviel went to her.

"Can I sit with you?" she asked.

The girl stared blankly past them, empty of all emotion, but her eyes conveyed a lifetime of tragedies most adults never experience.

Daeson watched as Raviel, with her beautiful soul, sat down next to her, quietly invading the space of this shattered little girl. She looked so weary of life already.

"What's your name?" Raviel asked quietly.

The girl slowly looked up at Raviel. "Petia." Her face was dirtied with smudges of soot. The few minor scratches on her face and arms belied the fatal wounds to her little heart.

"I'm Raviel, and he is Daeson."

Petia didn't take her eyes from Raviel. "They…they…my mother…my father…"

Her empty eyes filled with tears, and her lower lip began to quiver as Raviel wrapped an arm around her. Petia sank into Raviel's embraced and sobbed, her little shoulders shaking with each sorrowful cry. Raviel put a gentle hand on the girl's head and held her close.

Daeson had to look away, tears welling up. What monster of evil was the instrument of such pain and sorrow? Was he this monster?

He looked back at Raviel and she at him, their tears jointly crying out against the injustice.

After a long while, Petia fell asleep, her head resting on Raviel's lap. Daeson covered her with his pilot jacket and sat down beside Raviel. He looked down at Petia. She seemed to find temporary respite from her woe in sleep. Raviel gently stroked the girl's cheek, pushing hair away from her eyes.

Daeson glanced over at Raviel and then out the broken window just to his right. "What have I done, Raviel?" he whispered.

Daeson was staring at the carnage that had begun the night he entangled Raviel into his life and killed the sentry. Since that fateful night, there had been so much suffering...so much death. Now with the Plexus all but destroyed, these people had no hope. Both he and Raviel felt every tear and every drop of blood in gut-wrenching reality.

"So much sorrow for so many," Raviel whispered.

Daeson hung his head. Her words echoed over and over, bouncing off the walls of his mind yet not diminishing. *So much sorrow for so many!* The words were harsh, true, and horribly familiar. And in that moment of understanding, Daeson knew where to turn to find help to cope with this crushing burden of guilt.

"I must see the oracle."

Raviel looked up at him, her eyes void of life. "Why?"

"Because she told me this would happen, even before I knew I was Raylean. I want to know how she knew and why me. Where do I find her?"

Raviel turned and looked out over Drudgetown once again. She rested her head back on the concrete wall they were sitting against.

"You don't find the oracle; she finds you."

Daeson frowned. "That won't work. I want answers, and I'm not going to wait for them."

Raviel turned her gaze to Daeson, eyes weary.

"Don't you think these people want answers too?" she asked.

Daeson looked away. He deserved it, but coming from Raviel, the barb went deeper still. A moment later he felt her hand on his shoulder.

"I'm sorry, Daeson."

He didn't turn back. "No, I deserved that and much more. My selfishness did all of this, and now..." he turned and looked at Raviel. "And now my self-pity is ruining me further." He took a deep breath. "Perhaps she can give us answers that will help everyone."

"I truly don't know where to find Sabella. I've only heard rumors."

"A rumor is as good a place as any to start," Daeson said.

"On the western continent, there are many anti-graviton fields, and many of those hold up floating islands. It is said that she lives on one of those. But floating islands can be unstable, and navigating them is dangerous, which is why no one usually does."

Daeson nodded. "You're speaking of the Lamara Skies. Sounds like a perfect place for an oracle. Perhaps with a Starcraft we might have an advantage in our search and in our navigation of the anti-graviton fields."

Raviel looked down at Petia. She gently stroked the girl's brow and temple and then shook her head. "She has no one. I can't leave her here."

Daeson considered what that would mean for them, but he knew she was right. Petia was why they were here. The tragic life of this little girl symbolized every reason why they had come back.

"Then we'll bring her with us. It will complicate things, but—"

Raviel shook her head, unconvinced. "They tell me there's a refugee camp that's in desperate need of help." She looked at Daeson with eyes that told him she had made up her mind.

Daeson slowly nodded. "I understand."

Raviel leaned her head against the corner of the wall and closed her eyes. Daeson wanted to comfort her...hold her, but he dared not. Within minutes Raviel had drifted off to sleep.

The next day they carefully made their way out of the city and back into the country. During their two-day travel back to the Starcraft, Petia wouldn't let loose of Raviel's hand, but slowly the expanse of the open country seemed to help the broken little girl. Along the way they made their intent known to visit the refugee camp and to deliver any rations and medical supplies that the underground could offer. When they arrived back at the Starcraft, Rivet was standing guard, waiting for them, along with as many provisions as they could fit into the Starcraft's cargo bays.

"It is good to see you, my liege, and you, Lady Raviel." Rivet's calm voice soothed Daeson, and for the first time since having the machine join them, he felt at peace with it.

"It's good to see you too, Rivet," Daeson said.

Petia seemed mesmerized by the android. She went to Rivet and stood directly in front of him, staring up at the metallic marvel. At first Rivet seemed unaware, preoccupied with ensuring his liege and his lady were attended to. As Petia edged closer to Rivet, Daeson could tell that Raviel was nervous, reaching out for the little girl to take her hand. But Petia was undaunted and intrigued. She tilted her head as she examined the bot closely.

"Are you truly a robot?" Petia asked, staring up at the heartless machine.

Rivet looked down at Petia, his eyes cold and emotionless. The bot slowly knelt down to one knee so that he was eye to eye with her. Raviel moved closer, ready to scoop up her new charge at the first hint of danger, whether from ignorance *or* from mal-intent.

"Yes. I am Rivet, a maintenance service robot," Rivet said in his calm, emotionless voice. But to Daeson, there seemed to be a subtle measure of tenderness in the voice of the bot that he had not sensed before. Strange. Raviel eyed Rivet closely, but the bot held up his hand for Petia to touch. Petia didn't hesitate. She reached out and ran her fingers along the fingers of the bot, feeling each cold joint.

Then Petia looked up at Rivet and gazed into his optic sensors, as if she were peering into the soul of a real person. "*Just* a robot?"

Raviel's eyes grew wide. She shot a glance toward Daeson. He shook his head and held up his hand.

Rivet made one nod. "Yes, just a robot."

Petia then took both of her hands and grabbed each side of Rivet's head. Raviel moved closer but then she saw Petia smile. "I like you, Rivet. I think we will be friends."

Rivet stayed perfectly still until Petia let loose of his head and took Raviel's hand. Raviel scooped her up and away, not breaking her gaze from Rivet.

The bot looked at Raviel. "You need not worry, Lady Raviel. I am programmed to be careful around little ones."

Daeson stared at the bot in wonderment. Raviel said his programming was simple, yet Rivet was anything but that. Could such sophisticated programming be eloquently deceitful? In spite of Rivet's tender actions toward Petia, more questions had been raised about the bot's programming, ruining Daeson's peace once more. He tried to dismiss the historical accounts that testified to countless human atrocities caused by such intelligent machines, but he could not. In spite of the instances of Rivet's help and apparent loyalty, he and Raviel had no choice but to continue to be wary of the bot.

Before long, the odd quartet was flying toward the secret refugee camp. Rivet was stowed away in the cargo bay, and Petia was fastened to Raviel's lap in the second cockpit. The location of the camp was deep in the rugged terrain of the Abyssian Trenches. Daeson had a difficult time finding any place flat enough to land his Starcraft. He settled for a perch that was precarious but adequate. It was hard to imagine that anyone could survive in this desolate land, but it was perhaps the only place on Jypton for such a mass of desperate people to remain hidden. Makeshift shelters and caves housed thousands of displaced Rayleans, and once again, Daeson and Raviel were overwhelmed by the immense need. The supplies they brought were received with great enthusiasm.

The next day Daeson felt the urge to begin his search for the oracle. Raviel stood before him as Petia said goodbye to her mechanical friend.

"Tig is here for you, and I am told that Trisk is planning to rejoin with you any day now."

Raviel nodded but didn't seem encouraged. "I hope you find what you are looking for." She looked toward the camp and then back to Daeson. "They won't survive long here."

Daeson struggled with what else he could say to encourage her. He took a chance and reached for her hand. "I will be back."

Raviel's eyes were dim, and it nearly killed Daeson to see her this way. Being here to offer aid at the camp and having Petia to take care of offered some measure of purpose but did little to restore the force of life that she once owned.

Daeson turned toward the Starcraft, but Raviel held tightly to his hand. When he turned back to her, she reached up with her arm and wrapped it around his neck, her cheek pressing against his. He waited for her message in his ear, but there was none. His heart pounded as he carefully hugged her until she released him, and as she did, she turned away.

"Come, Petia."

Petia smiled at the bot kneeling before her. She leaned toward him and whispered something in his ear and then ran to Raviel, taking her hand.

I shouldn't have done that, Raviel thought. She wondered if perhaps it was more for herself than it was for Daeson. Her heart hurt so badly. It reminded her of the day Aliza died—the overwhelming grief with no escape and no hope. She was struggling to even carry on. With the likely fate of her parents, it seemed that everyone she cared about was being removed from her life. Raviel felt the little tug on her hand and looked down. Petia seemed to sense Raviel's pain. Her compassionate smile lit up her sweet face.

"He loves you," Petia said matter-of-factly. "I can tell."

Raviel tried to smile, but it would not come.

"Do you love him?" Petia continued. "That I can't tell."

Raviel hesitated. What a simple but hard question. *Did she?* She stopped to lift Petia up on to a large rocky outcropping they had to traverse in order to get back to the camp. She set the girl on the ledge, but Petia held on to Raviel's arms, looking her right in the eyes as if to analyze her face for an answer.

Raviel formed a weak smile. "I can't," she finally responded. "He's a lost soul, Petia. One day you'll understand."

Petia tilted her head and then Raviel joined her on the ledge to continue their trek back.

The truth was that Raviel wanted to love him, and her feelings could not be quenched. It was why she had reached for him when they parted. There was the chance she would never see him again, and the thought of one more thing to regret was too much. But her actions had only made everything worse, teasing her heart with something she could never have. And above all was the lingering hopelessness. The Plexus, their best and only hope for breaking out from under the oppression of the Jyptonians, was essentially gone—destroyed. Now they were all condemned to execution or never-ending slavery.

As she and Petia drew near to the camp, she looked over her shoulder to see Daeson's Starcraft accelerate upward and away. The distant rumble oddly soothed her. Even if he found answers for himself, what good would it do now? They had waited too long. The desperation of her people was too great. Yes, she was angry with Daeson, but what of Ell Yon? Was she guilty of Daeson's accusations...of believing in a non-existent Immortal that had been fabricated in the minds of a hopelessly enslaved people? Such thoughts were crushing, but how could she not think this way in such desperate times?

"Ell Yon will find him." Petia's voice shook Raviel from her sober contemplation. She looked down at the little girl. "If he is lost, then Ell Yon will find him. That's what Ell Yon does, isn't it?"

Raviel pulled Petia's head to her thigh and hugged her, mostly to keep her from seeing the tears that threatened to spill. Petia's one small statement held all of Raviel's dearest hopes.

"Human emotions are a curious thing," Rivet said as they watched Raviel and Petia walk away.

"How so?" Daeson asked, wondering what a programmed computer would have to say about something it could never experience or understand.

Rivet turned his head to look at Daeson. "It seems you often say that which you shouldn't, and you do not say that which you should."

"Really?" Daeson replied. "And is that merely an observation or a judgment?"

"Merely an observation, my liege. But the greatest mystery of all is how the emotions of love evoke actions that do not make sense and are neither justifiable. I have learned to be careful around humans that exhibit such symptoms."

Daeson raised an eyebrow. "You are wise beyond your programming, Rivet. Let's go."

Daeson and Rivet strapped into the Starcraft and were soon skimming across the Marricoo Ocean toward the western continent and the Lamara Skies. Daeson had no idea where to begin looking, but he was willing to do whatever it took to find the white-haired oracle. She knew too much, and more than that, she seemed to hold the key to his future and perhaps the future of all Rayleans—if there was one.

EPILOGUE

A Distant Future

"You can't stop there, Dad!" Brae urged in exasperation, as she sat up and looked at her father.

Elias smiled. "It's late beyond reason, Brae, and you have tech classes tomorrow. As it is, you're going to have a hard time keeping your eyes open."

Brae's shoulders dropped as she sighed. "I suppose you're right. But promise me you'll finish the story tomorrow," she pleaded as she grabbed his hand.

"Of course...or perhaps the next day when you've gotten enough sleep."

"Deal!"

Inside Brae's bedroom, Elias tucked her in bed and kissed her forehead.

"Sleep fast and sleep well."

Brae smiled. "I will," she replied, but her mind was filled with brilliant images of the story of Daeson and Raviel. It would take some time to tame her thoughts before sleep would come. Never before had the story of the ancients felt so real to her. Her world and the galaxy itself seemed different with each passing year, leaving her to contemplate the way the fabric of fantasy and pretend was slowly melting into the reality of her future…a future that she felt was somehow connected to the stories of her forefathers.

Elias walked to the door and motioned for the light to diminish.

"Dad?" Brae called after him.

Elias turned.

"It's not just a story, is it?"

Elias hesitated.

"No, Brae. It's not."

For some inexplicable reason, Brae felt an emotional rush well up within her. Perhaps it was that for the very first time, she actually believed these tales of victory and woe had happened to real people with real emotions—people like her.

"I love you, Dad."

"I love you too, Brae."

AUTHOR'S COMMENTARY

The canvas of life upon which God has given us the ability to create stories is truly remarkable—a limitless universe, emotions, senses, a world of unrepeatable humans, and minds to imagine untold adventures. My greatest concern in the writing of this series is my limited human ability to appropriately represent the God of the Bible through the use of metaphors.

Please do not make the mistake of assuming that science and technology can in some way explain away God: His supernatural marvels, His holiness, His power, His wisdom, and His love. The full character of God is unknowable; thus, attempting to depict Him in all of His glory is a frightful endeavor. I pray that you will return to His Word and fully embrace the profound descriptions of truth found there, expressed without the limitations of fiction.

It is my purpose in writing these words to point you once more to the glorious God of love, His Son Jesus Christ, the Holy Spirit, and the radical intersection of supernatural love through the redemptive power of the gospel.

~Chuck Black

ABOUT THE AUTHOR

Chuck Black graduated from North Dakota State University with a degree in Electrical and Electronic Engineering. After traveling the world as a tactical combat communications engineer for the United States Air Force, he was accepted into pilot training and served the nation as an F-16 fighter pilot. He is the author of twenty-two novels, including the popular *Kingdom Series, The Knights of Arrethtrae* series, the *Wars of the Realm* series, *The Starlore Legacy* series, and *Call to Arms: The Guts and Glory of Courageous Fatherhood. Kingdom's Dawn* was on CBA's top ten best sellers list twice in 2008 for all Christian Youth Literature.

Chuck is also an entrepreneur with sixteen patents and is currently the president and general manager for FlowCore Systems, a chemical injection automation company in the oil and gas industry located in Williston, North Dakota.

Chuck is a believer in Jesus Christ as Lord and Savior and in the Holy-Spirit-inspired, infallible Word of God. He is devoted to his wife, Andrea, their six children and spouses, and numerous grandchildren. It is his desire to inspire people of all ages to follow the Lord with zeal and to equip parents, pastors, and youth leaders to accomplish the same through his allegorical and Scripture-based novels, seminars, podcast, and published articles.

CHUCK BLACK

THE STARLORE LEGACY

FLIGHT

EPISODE **TWO**

THE STARLORE  LEGACY

FLIGHT

Ancient prophecies promise a future of hope, but who dares face the wrath of a powerful tyrant?

Daeson seeks the counsel of the oracle that propelled him into a life of ruin and terrifying adventure. But the ruthless Chancellor Lockridge offers no quarter to his life-long friend turned traitor. Lockridge's thirst for revenge spills the blood of thousands of innocent Rayleans, and Daeson bears the burden of global calamity. Rejected by all except the spirited Raviel, Daeson struggles to carry on. When the whispers of the Immortal Ell Yon beckon Daeson to a remote moon of the planet Mesos, he must find the courage to face his deepest fears. Can Daeson trust the words of an ancient Immortal and inspire the slaves of Jypton to rise up? Not only does the future of his people hang in the balance, but the entire galaxy as well!

Published by
Perfect Praise Publishing
Williston, ND

CHUCK BLACK

THE STARLORE LEGACY

LORE

EPISODE **THREE**

THE STARLORE  LEGACY
LORE

**The Raylean people teeter on the edge of annihilation.
Can Daeson lead the quest for their promised homeworld?**

Daeson finds himself a prisoner in a tribal world where the law of survival rules. Gone is the hope of the promised homeworld given by the mighty Immortal, Ell Yon. Daeson must fight to restore a future to the Raylean people, but to succeed he must overcome the marauders of cruel worlds, the tragedy of quantum peril, and the arch-enemy of the Sovereign Ell Yon, Lord Dracus. The odds are mounting against him. The relentless loyalty of his friend, Tig, sustains him as he rediscovers the power of the Protector. Can he lead the Rayleans to freedom once more?

Published by
Perfect Praise Publishing
Williston, ND –

PERFECT PRAISE
PUBLISHING

ALL RIGHTS RESERVED